THE
MANATEE
DID
IT

SOUTHERN
BEACH
MYSTERIES
1

THE
MANATEE
DID
IT

KAY DEW SHOSTAK

Kay Dew Shostak

THE MANATEE DID IT
Copyright © 2020 by Kay Dew Shostak.
All rights reserved.

ISBN: 978-0-9991064-9-5

SOUTHERN FICTION: Cozy Mystery / Southern Mystery / Florida Mystery / Island Mystery / Empty Nest Mystery / Clean Mystery / Small Town Mystery

Text Layout and Cover Design
by Roseanna White Designs
Cover Images from www.Shutterstock.com

Author photo by Susan Eason with www.EasonGallery.com

Published by August South Publishing. You may contact the publisher at:
AugustSouthPublisher@gmail.com

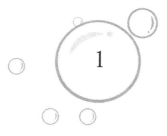

1

"We saw a manatee here under the dock last week," the short woman on my right says as she holds one hand above her eyes to block the midafternoon sun. "We first thought it was an old tire. They're big and kind of float right below the surface." She leans forward on her tiptoes and looks over the railing. She's joined by me and three other women, all around the same age. What age? Well, let's just say none of us needed to hire a babysitter to go to lunch today, unless it was for a grandkid.

"Funny how before we ate lunch all that fried seafood smelled so yummy, but now, not so much," the heaviest of the women opines. She leans over, looking into the marina water on my other side, her armful of bangle bracelets jangling. "So glad you joined our lunch group,

Jewel. It was a smaller group today with only nine of us, but it varies each week. Lucy got your email address, so you're on our list, right?"

I nod, smile, and say "yes", but as I look at our reflections in the dark green water, not one of their names comes to mind. I used to quickly remember names whenever and wherever we moved, but not this time. Not in this fog. I want to say I look forward to these lunches and to making new friends, but the words just won't come. I bend my head toward the water, letting the sides of my shoulder-length hair fall between me and the other ladies.

Sounds of the restaurant to our left cover the silence. Colby's Seafood Café sits high on pilings in the middle of Sophia Beach's marina. The marina is on the river side of Sophia Island, an Atlantic barrier island on the north coast of Florida. Both the marina and the café are long-time favorites with locals and tourists. Sophia Beach is the little town settled around the riverside marina on the island. And—insert drumroll here— the new home of Jewel and Craig Mantelle. I think brightly and try to force some positivity into my thoughts. The *new* home of Jewel and Craig Mantelle!

However, a tear slips down my face and drops to the water below. *Enough of this!* I laugh, not caring if it sounds fake, and stand up straight. My voice is as shrill as my laugh. "I'd love to see a manatee. Of all the places we've lived, we've never lived anywhere that had manatees."

The big woman with curly, silver hair pats my back, her bangle bracelets rattling. "I bet moving is hard, but you'll find good things here." She winks at me and exudes pure joy when she says, "Like us!"

I swallow and force sincerity into my smile. They all return my smile, and then we turn away from the railing, talking about afternoon plans.

"How about you, Jewel? What are you doing this afternoon?" the woman closest to me asks. She's tall and doesn't have the Southern accent of the other three women.

"I'm still unpacking—this afternoon, tomorrow afternoon, every afternoon for the rest of my life it feels like," I moan, but I remember to smile. When I pause for just a second, my smile slips into a look of embarrassment, and adding a deep sigh, I confess. "Would you mind reminding me of your names again? I'm so sorry. I guess it's the move that's gotten my memory so fuzzy."

The lady with the silver curls laughs. "Shoot, wish I had a move to blame my forgetfulness on, but nope, I've lived here all my life. All sixty-six years of it, still can't remember a thing. I'm Annie, don't worry about last names yet." Annie's silver curls are so beautiful they look like a wig, but they aren't. I've already looked close enough to check.

"My name is Cherry." The tall, non-Southern lady with short, dark hair waves at me. "We only moved here five years ago when my husband retired. I'm a nurse, and I work at the hospital here on the island on the weekends. I'm parked up in town," she adds as she stops walking at the edge of the parking lot.

The petite woman who'd seen the manatee last week nods to the lady beside her. "Charlotte and I drove together, and we found a spot just the next row over." She sticks her hand out at me. "And I'm Tamela. Retired from teaching just last month, so I'm enjoying getting to do things like our weekly lunches for more than just the summer."

I shake her hand. "I'm a teacher, too, but we moved around so much it was hard to get into a school system. I haven't taught in years. So, you're Charlotte," I say, turning to the remaining woman.

"Yes, Charlotte Bellington. We actually live near each other. I knew your husband's aunt Cora. Such a shame, don't you think?" Easily the oldest woman of the group, Charlotte also looks the most formidable, wearing such an intense scowl that she completely catches me off guard.

"Oh." My gulp is followed by stammering. "Oh, well… that's nice. I, uh, I didn't know her. I, uh…"

Tamela waves a hand toward me and says, "It's okay, honey, we know. Charlotte, let's go if you still want to stop by the library." Tamela puts her hand under Charlotte's arm as they step off the curbed sidewalk along the docks.

Cherry, the nurse, rolls her eyes behind their backs and turns to me. "Jewel, just ignore Charlotte. She thinks she owns this town."

Annie shrugs. "Well, she kinda does, but don't let her get your panties in a wad. She's a good soul underneath it all." She pats the hood of the car beside her. "I snagged a spot right here today. It's getting busier and busier down here at lunchtime. I'm off to the grocery," she says as she presses her key fob and the car beeps. "Good to meet you, Jewel. See you next Wednesday."

Cherry straightens her shoulders and puts sunglasses on. "I'm parked a couple blocks up Centre Street. I want to stop in the bookstore. Have a good afternoon." She pauses and leans back toward me, grasping my forearm. "It'll all settle out before long. This group is a good way to meet people, so be sure and come next week."

"Oh, I'm already looking forward to it. My husband, Craig, is out of town until Friday, then leaves again Sunday night." I quickly clamp down on my bottom lip to keep it from trembling.

Cherry squeezes my arm. "That stinks just moving here and him traveling so much, but maybe it'll calm down soon?"

"Not likely. He was supposed to be retiring early, but then this project came up, and, well…" I look around and sigh, which with my lip trembling sounds downright mournful. "It's our first move without the kids, so it's strange."

Cherry pats my arm. "That is hard. It was the same for us when we moved here, but it'll be all right. I promise." She straightens up and sighs. "Guess I'd better get going. Where'd you park?"

"On the other side of the restaurant." Trying another smile, I step back. "I think I'll just walk on down the dock instead of through the parking lot. And thanks for the pep talk. It'll be okay. I know. It always is." With another bigger smile, I veer back to walk closer to the railing, looking over the edge at the dark green water of the river. It feels good to relax my face; forced smiles use weird muscles. Then my breath catches, and I yell, "Hey, uh, Cherry! Look it's a manatee!" I point toward the water.

Cherry turns, then motions to Annie, who is still sitting in her car looking at her phone. Cherry yells, "Jewel sees a manatee!" and jogs across the parking lot. Annie struggles out of her compact car, then slams the door, hurrying after the more limber Cherry.

Cherry rests her hands on her hips and grins at her friend, shouting, "Well, come on, Grandma. Although I guess we won't miss anything since we actually still move a *little* bit faster than a manatee."

As they come to stand on either side of me at the railing, I point down. "See? Across there by the dock pilings, coming out from the shadows. Just below the surface. Wait…"

Cherry pulls off her sunglasses and squints at the dark water under the dock across from us. "I don't see anything."

Annie blocks the sun from her eyes. Then as waves from a passing boat begin bouncing the boats and the floating dock across from us, she exclaims, "There! I see it."

I pull my phone out of my pocket. "Gotta get a picture. The kids won't believe I saw a manatee. There it comes, see it?"

We watch as a rolling wave pushes the manatee into the sunshine. Instead of gray, though, it's more of a tan color. Actually, khaki. And white.

And human.

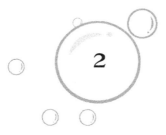

2

Shouts and pounding steps on the dock jar us as we lift our heads and stare at each other. By the time we look back at the scene, people are already pulling the facedown man out of the water. Cherry warns, "Girls, I'd look away if I were you. You do not want to see a drowning victim's face, especially if the fish have already gotten to him."

Annie and I immediately turn around. All three of us cross the dock and plop down onto one of the benches placed there for river sunset viewing. We can see the action around the man, but it is a little removed behind the railings. Then, as the crowd grows, we can't see the victim at all. Taking in the running and shouting, we sit quietly for a few moments.

"Wonder who it is?" Annie asks just above a

whisper. Then she sighs and her voice is steadi-
er. "Hope it's a stranger. That sounds awful to
say, but lots of folks from all over dock here for
lunch or to shop. Sad, but I don't want it to be
someone I know. You know?"

Cherry nods, then shrugs. "Of course, but
there aren't as many visitors lately with the shape
the marina's in from the last few hurricanes."
She turns around at the sound of a siren. "Here
come the police and ambulance, though I don't
believe any resuscitation will help. That's why I
didn't offer any assistance."

Annie stands up. "This place is going to get
crazier than a zoo. I'm leaving so I don't get my
car stuck here with all the emergency vehicles."

"Good idea," Cherry says as she also stands.
"Jewel, there's an exit for the parking lot you're
in on the other side of Colby's. I'd suggest going
out that direction."

I also get up, but then hesitate. "You don't
think we need to stay? Talk to the police?"

"We didn't see anything more than all those
other folks," Cherry explains. "Even all the people in the restaurant saw what we saw. They'll
probably have more eyewitness reports than
they can deal with."

"Probably true. It seems sad to just leave,

but…" My words trail off as we walk toward the parking lot again.

Annie plods along behind us. "I agree, but there's nothing we can do. Most likely some-one had a heart attack and fell off their boat. We can read all about it in the paper on Friday. Or on Facebook in just a few more minutes, where we'll get more details than hanging out here. I'm anxious to find out who it is." She steps up to walk next to me and lays her arm across my shoulders. "You look like you need another hug," she says with a low laugh as she squeezes me. Letting me go she whispers, "Besides, spot-ting a dead body is *way* more unusual than see-ing a manatee!"

Cherry turns around as she keeps walking and groans. "Oh, Annie. You're awful." She picks up her pace and waves. "See you later, ladies!"

Annie steps over to her car while I angle away from her through the parking lot, having lost all interest in walking along the docks on the way back to my parking place. It's hard to see the water even when the dock isn't lined with rubberneckers and emergency crews. Chain-link fencing blocks off damaged parts of the dock. From what Cherry said, it's damage due to past hurricanes. Before we moved Craig said this area never got hit by hurricanes.

Apparently he was wrong.

My path takes me up near Colby's Café, which is built higher than the docks. From that vantage point I stop to watch as more emergency personnel arrive. I stretch to see if the man from the water is visible, but all I see is the crowd around him. However, no one seems to be in a hurry, which pretty much verifies Cherry's professional opinion that the man is dead.

Turning away, I weave through the outside tables, full of chattering patrons, then walk down the other side, headed toward my car. The parking lot is crowded with others leaving like myself, but there are possibly even more arriving, drawn to the commotion. With a shudder I realize it'll be a long time before I look down off those docks and don't picture those khaki pants, that white shirt and bald head.

The exit Cherry mentioned at the other end of the lot has a long line of cars, so it's easy to find. When it's finally my turn, after nearly fifteen minutes waiting, I ease onto the road, turning to the right and away from Centre Street with all its shops and restaurants and traffic. Unlike all those little dots on the map that get historic downtown status to hopefully attract tourists to a couple old buildings filled with junk, Sophia Beach is a truly historic downtown on historic Sophia Island.

Carnegies, Vanderbilts, and DuPonts were only a few of the famous families and individuals who visited the island on their yachts before railroads made travel to Florida easier. Shops and restaurants fill the old buildings on Centre Street as it heads down to the marina. In the few weeks we've lived here, I've come to love driving and walking on Centre, but not today as I try to stay on the edge of all the excitement. Just a couple blocks to my right, and I'm out of the business area, driving under a canopy of old oak trees draped in Spanish moss. Farther back, underneath those ancient trees, sit houses with deep porches, elaborate railings, and tall windows.

For so many years I've sought out little towns like this as we moved around the nation. I even subscribed to magazines full of the graceful living happening in old homes on shaded streets like these. Of course I dreamed of what it would be like living in one of the old homes, but never—never—did I expect to see those fantasies come true. Craig isn't really a handyman type, and we've never had the kind of money needed to restore an old home.

Passing almost a block of wrought iron fencing, I slow to a crawl as I come to the open gate and turn into the sandy driveway on my right. The driveway is lined with six tall palms on each side, leading to two levels of deep porches, more elaborate railings, and dozens of tall windows. The only difference between this house and the others is that it's bigger than most of them.

Oh yeah, and I live here.

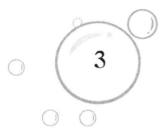

3

Corabelle Mantelle Hocking's childhood home was built by her grandfather, Howard Mantelle Senior, in 1888. That much I'd read on the historical marker out by the sidewalk—I'm still wrapping my head around the fact that we live in a house with its own historical marker. Howard had been in shipping and commissioned this mansion for his large family. He died in 1915, leaving a dozen adult children living around the area, but his wife alone in the huge mansion.

According to the marker, Howard Junior moved in with his new bride in 1915, and his mother, the original Corabelle Mantelle, died in 1920. Howard and his brothers ran Mantelle Shipping, which the historical marker points out was a formidable enterprise and responsible for much of the area's growth. However, the marker ends by saying that family strife tore the business apart around the time of the Great Depression.

Craig's aunt Corabelle was born in 1922—I saw her birthdate on one of the legal documents that brought us here—and grew up in the mansion. She was the older of two children raised here, and we found a couple pictures of the young family in the front bedroom: one at the seashore and one in a studio. I want to have them cleaned and framed, but the rest of her story is so sad I'm not sure I will. Shortly after her wedding, her brother, Howard the Third, and her new husband died in a sailing accident. Craig says he never heard what happened to her parents as she wouldn't talk about anything having to do with family. He only remembered that detail about her husband dying when I asked why she hadn't left the house to her own children. He kept repeating that she was a recluse and, like his mother, wouldn't talk about family. Craig doesn't like talking about family either. At least I know where he got that from.

Craig's mother, Jaqueline, raised him alone, and he still knows nothing about his father. Jaqueline died when our children were little, and I never got to know her. She liked to keep to herself and wasn't close to her son, so I didn't push. Besides, I was busy with the twins before I got used to having a husband, much less a mother-in-law across the country.

Carefully picking my way up the wide, front steps to avoid the rotten sections, my heaviness at living in this place, and this house, returns. This hot, strange place. This broken-down, moldy, dark house. The excitement and shock of Craig inheriting his Aunt Cora's home right as we were contemplating retirement completely evaporated after only one month of living here.

"It was like it was meant to be. Should've seen all the red flags, but nope. Not us!" I mutter to the temperamental, heavy front door. I fit the old key in the keyhole and push it, just right, with my shoulder. "Sight unseen. Have to sign the papers within the week. No time to see what we're getting. It's an adventure!"

My nose automatically wrinkles crossing the threshold. Mold. Mildew. Dust. Now I can talk to myself more loudly as I do day after day here. Sometimes I do it to ward off the loneliness, sometimes to cover the creepy noises of an old house. "Not enough vanilla candles in the world to cover that." I drop my purse onto one of the tables lining the walls of the entrance. "Yep. So, here it is. Our retirement adventure, except like most of our life together, I'm doing it all alone."

The darkness of the porch allows my eyes to quickly adjust to the dimness of the entryway and downstairs rooms. I literally shake my head to drown out the pity party gathering there, and I stop in the wide entrance to the living room. I lift my shoulders, straighten my back, and place my fists on my hips, saying even louder, "Today I'm tearing down those curtains. I'm not waiting on an appraiser or Craig's approval. *I'm* the one that has to live in this dungeon all day, every day!"

"Jewel? Who are you talking to?"

"Oh! Craig!" I bend over with my hands clasped to my chest. "You scared me to death! What are you doing here?" My hands don't leave my pounding heart, though I do try to stand up straight.

"Sorry," he says as he takes a step toward me. "Hitch in permitting meant no work for a couple days, so I thought I'd come back here. I sent you a text this morning. Didn't you see my car?"

"I silenced my phone for lunch, and I started parking out by the front sidewalk. No reason I can see for pulling all the way around the house. It's not like having a car in front of it can hurt this place's curb appeal," I say with a certain nasty sarcasm that seems to creep into my voice these days. I grimace at him, but he just laughs.

"No, I guess you're right." Craig's hair has only started turning gray, and he's as trim as he's always been. Being on the jobsite in Florida has already given him a tan. People say we look good together, but I think this move has given me more wrinkles and a bad attitude while his new tan makes him look younger. Of course he's not stuck in this place day after day. And, no, I'm not bitter—much. I work to turn my grimace into a smile, lower the shoulders that keep creeping up around my ears, and walk across the uneven, water-damaged floor to welcome my husband home with a quick kiss.

As I step away from him, I look at the windows and say, "The curtains."

He follows my look. "The curtains?"

"That's who I was talking to. They've got to go." I lay a hand on his shoulder and sigh. "I went to lunch with those ladies and—oh!" I pull away from him and start pacing the entryway.

This isn't easy even though the entryway is massive. The entire downstairs entertaining area is crowded with Aunt Cora's little tables, which are further loaded with knickknacks. There are side tables, end tables, coffee tables, phone tables. There are porcelain dolls, bronzed baby shoes, and in one instance, a toy from a Happy Meal. Some of this junk is possibly quality antique. Other pieces are definitely not, I would think, but who knows.

"You are not going to believe what happened," I say as I weave around a table with an inlaid checkerboard pattern. The Precious Moments figurine atop it wobbles threateningly. "After lunch we came out, you know there on the docks beside Colby's? Well, I thought I saw a manatee."

"Oh, cool," he says as he unbuttons the sleeves of his shirt.

I stop him and explain. "No, not cool. It wasn't a manatee." I swallow. "It was a body. A man. He was, he was dead."

Craig stops with one sleeve unbuttoned. His mouth falls open. "What! You found a body? Who was it? What happened?"

I walk past him down the hall to the kitchen. "I don't know. We left. All the police and firemen were there." I pull open the refrigerator and take out a bottle of water. "It was crazy. Annie, she's one of the ladies from lunch, thinks someone probably had a heart attack and fell off their boat."

When Craig joins me in the kitchen, I hold out the water to him. He takes the bottle, then leans against the center bar in the big kitchen.

"That's incredible. Sorry you had to go through that. How crazy."

"Yes, crazy and definitely creepy, but other than that, lunch was fun. I'm glad you encouraged me to go. This place," I rake my eyes around the dark and cluttered house, "gets overwhelming after a while."

The kitchen was one of the first rooms I'd attacked. I threw away the clutter (who needs three ancient can openers?) and old food and cleaned, so it, along with our bedroom and bathroom upstairs, was actually livable. But only just. Worn-out linoleum floors, dated countertops, and stained and cracked porcelain have to be overlooked in the kitchen and bathroom, but the rooms *are* clean. As clean as an ancient, neglected house can possibly be.

Pounding on the front door makes us both jump. Craig winces as he says, "Oh, yeah, the doorbell doesn't work, does it?"

Craig wrenches open the front door as I join him there. "Hello," he says to the two police officers standing on our porch.

"Mr. and Mrs. Mantelle?" one of the officers asks.

"Yes?"

"Hello. I'm Officer Greyson, and this is my partner, Officer Bryant. I don't think your doorbell works," the officer says. I can't help but notice that both he and his younger partner are trying to look beyond us to the inside of the house. "Can we come in? We need to ask you some questions, Mrs. Mantelle."

"Me?" I take a step back, then nod. "Oh, yes. The marina. The body." I back up, waving a hand toward the living room. "Yes, come in."

The officer's eyes stop their roving and laser in on me, but he catches himself and follows my invitation into the large, dark-paneled room. Craig pushes the front door shut, then joins us.

"Mrs. Mantelle, did you say 'the body'?" Officer Greyson asks me.

"Yes, in the water. I was with some ladies, and we saw it. Then others got there and pulled it out. We didn't stay any longer. One of the ladies I was with is a nurse, and she said we didn't want to see a drowning victim."

The younger officer stands a step behind his partner. He takes out a notepad and pen for his first addition to the conversation. "Ma'am, can you give me the names of the ladies you were with?"

"Of course. Cherry and Annie, but we just moved here so I don't know their last names."

The older officer closes his eyes for a moment, then, opening them, he stretches his neck like he has a headache. With his head bent to the side he asks, "You just moved here, yet this is called the Mantelle House and you *are* the Mantelles."

Craig nods as he answers. "Yes, I inherited the house from my aunt. She had been sick for a long time. In a nursing facility for quite a while. We were estranged, I guess you could say. It was rather a surprise. The inheritance, that is."

The two uniformed men look around at the place, and I look away. *No need to see their pity.* "Would you gentlemen like to sit down?" I perch on one of the several side chairs in the room. There are also several couches, one of which is oozing its stuffing. And don't forget the tables. When the officers don't sit down, Craig doesn't either.

Officer Greyson continues. "Mrs. Mantelle, you were at the marina today. Said you were there for lunch? What time was that?"

"Well, I got there a little early, so I was wandering around looking at the water. I didn't know the other women, so I didn't want to get to the table early. The sun got hot on the docks. I'm not used to this kind of weather in March. It's still winter where we came from. Anyway, I went over to a bench next to the restaurant in

the shade and sat down. I finally went inside at
ten minutes till noon."

Both officers seem very focused when Officer
Greyson asks, "Did you talk to anyone?"

I think, then shake my head. "No, I was
alone on the bench."

"How about before you sat down on the
bench?"

"Um, no. I'd parked on the other side and
walked around along the dock. But there's no
boats on that side, I guess due to the hurricane
damage, so I went around to see the boats. And,
well, to waste time like I said." I smile up at
the officers, but they don't smile back. I look at
Craig and shrug. He steps over to put a hand on
my shoulder and gives me a small squeeze.

"Is this what you were wearing?" the younger
officer asks, pointing at me with his pen.

I look down at my red cotton sweater, white
jeans, and leather sandals. "Yes, why?"

"And you talked to no one?" the younger officer asks again.

"Not that I remember. I was nervous about
meeting all these strangers for lunch. I wandered
around, and I did ask this man there about the
sunset cruises. He was beside the sign and for
some reason looked like he might know. Are you
talking about him?"

I chew on my bottom lip and squint, trying to remember the man. He had on a hat, and when he took it off to wipe his brow, he was bald. Like the man in the water. And, wait, he had on khaki pants. Like the man in the water. My head jerks up as my heart races. "But, he had on a Hawaiian shirt. It was one of those bright ones, with flowers and palm leaves! It couldn't have been him. Right?" I slowly rise and stare at the officers.

The officers look at each other and frown. The older one says, "Ma'am, you're going to need to remember everything he said and that you said. Maybe we should sit down." He sighs and rubs his mouth, which sets in a line. "This might take a while."

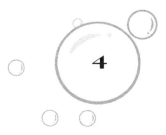

4

Before we can sit down, the younger officer's phone chimes, the same setting I use for an alarm. He apparently has it set for someone special as he doesn't even look at it before he starts walking toward the front door, saying, "I'll take this outside."

The phone continues to chime as Officer Bryant faces down our front door. We think the warming weather has made the wood swell so that it's almost impossible to jerk open.

I feel weird giving an officer of the law advice, but he looks so helpless standing there with xylophone chimes continuing to play out of his phone. "Um, you—you pull up and then out," I say.

The officer whips around. It looks like he has to work to soften the frustration from his features. "I've got it, ma'am." He sighs and unlocks his phone, puts it to his ear. "Hold on a second, Mother."

Craig and I share a look. *Mother?*

Finally, Officer Bryant muscles the door open with a triumphant "Ha!" He pulls it shut, but it won't close all the way without some special tugging, so we won't have to get up to let him in.

I really am starting to hate that door.

Officer Greyson actually rolls his eyes, which causes Craig and me to look at each other again as we all take a seat. The officer is on the burgundy velvet couch, or settee, as some people call it. I return to my chair, and Craig pulls another chair close to mine. We haven't arranged any furniture yet as we don't know what we're keeping. Again, appraisal first? Cleaning first? It's anyone's call.

Officer Greyson looks toward the front door where his partner can be heard talking. His mouth presses into disapproval. I probably shouldn't ask, but… "Does his mother call him often at work?"

The officer looks at me, rolls his eyes again, and moves on. "Now, Mrs. Mantelle, this man you talked to, can you be more specific as to what was said?"

"Of course. I asked him if he knew anything about the different river cruises that were advertised on the placard there on the dock. He said not really, but he'd seen them come and go full of people who looked happy. I asked where they left from, and he pointed to the ramp there at the end. Then he pointed to where two of the boats would regularly be docked, but they were out on tours over on that island. Can't remember the name, but it's a park?"

Craig and the officer say at the same time, "Cumberland."

"Right, with the wild horses. Anyway, then he said for me to have a good day and walked away."

"Which direction?"

"Toward the restaurant. But then I turned the other way and walked along the railing for a bit before turning around and going to sit on the bench like I told you." We all turn to the front door as it pushes open. I can't help but smile at the redness of the young officer's face. Imagine his mother calling him at work. I remind myself to not do that to my kids anymore—unless it's something important, of course.

Craig and I both jump when Officer Greyson demands of the young man, "Okay, what is it now? Was it her? It was, wasn't it?"

With a sigh, the officer sits down beside his partner. He finally looks at him and nods.

"I knew it! Great." Officer Greyson frowns and shakes his head, then points to Craig and me. "Go ahead. Tell 'em."

My stomach clinches. I press my folded arms close to my body to try and hide a shiver. I usually have trouble keeping warm, but I especially have trouble with it when I'm scared. And they've scared me with all this.

Officer Bryant takes a deep breath and coughs. "Well, ma'am, my mother. Um, yeah, well, Annie is my mother. Annie Bryant."

"My Annie? I mean, the Annie from lunch?"

"Yes, ma'am. And so she called me to say that you were with her during the time that—well, during the time we're looking at."

Craig lets out his breath with a little laugh. "Oh, okay. That's good. Right?"

"Wait, how did she even know you were over here?" I ask.

Annie's son lowers his head. Officer Greyson rolls his eyes again and explains. "Officer Bryant's mother has to know everything that happens in Sophia, and even with the resorts and all the growth, this is really just a very small town. *Everyone knows* we're here. When you said you were with someone named Annie today, we knew with our luck that it was her." He growls under his breath. "This is less like a partnership than a trio with his mother as our third wheel." He stands up and looks around. "Always wanted to see what this place looked like on the inside." He reaches out a hand to shake Craig's hand, then mine. "Welcome to Sophia Beach. Mrs. Mantelle, if you think of anything else, give us a call. Bryant, give her one of your cards. We know Annie would never let her call me."

His face returning to a more normal color, the young officer hands me a card. "I'm Aiden Bryant. My mom said you were a nice lady, and she'll be talking to you soon."

From near the front door Officer Greyson scoffs. "Soon? Try she's probably on her way here now. Nice to meet you folks."

Aiden bobs his reddening face and hurries after his partner.

Craig closes the door behind the officers and lets out a breath. I rush to him and hug him tight. "I'm so glad you were here today. What if you hadn't come home early? They were nice, but, well, I'm just glad you were here."

He grasps my upper arms and holds me out so he can see my face. "You do have to remember, like he said, this is a very small town. We've not lived in many small towns." He hugs me again and mumbles into my hair. "I'd forgotten exactly how small this place is."

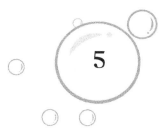

5

Before the hug ends there's another knock on the door. I smile at him and pull away. "Think that's Annie?"

He shrugs, and I walk to the door. I tug it open, and there she stands. Well, there she stood for about half a second, before she rushed in.

"Can you believe this?" she exclaims as she passes me. "Oh, you must be Jewel's husband. I'm Annie Bryant." Then she turns to me. "I thought you said he was out of town?"

"My work plans changed. Craig Mantelle," Craig says, holding out his hand. "Nice to meet you, but I do have some work to do. Can I get you ladies something to drink?"

Annie shakes his hand, saying, "A glass of ice water would be wonderful. Aren't you glad you came home on such an exciting day?"

My husband laughs, but raises his eyebrows at me as he turns for the kitchen. "Water for you, too, Jewel?"

"Sure, thanks. Annie, we got to meet your son. He's very nice. You must be so proud of him."

"Of course. He's the youngest of my boys. Should we sit in here?"

"Okay. As you can see, you have your choice of places to sit."

"My, my. Always wanted to see the inside of this place," she says, echoing Officer Greyson. "Kind of musty, ain't it? Cora was a strange duck indeed. You didn't know her, did you? Well, I hope this old furniture will hold my big behind!" she says with a laugh as she settles into the middle of the same small couch her son and his partner sat on.

I sit back down where I was as Craig brings us each a glass of water. "Here you go. Now I need to make some phone calls, so I'm going to barricade myself in my office for a bit. You ladies enjoy. Nice to meet you, Mrs. Bryant."

"Oh, no, I'm Annie," she says. "Mrs. Bryant is my mother-in-law, and she doesn't share her name or, truth be told, anything else!"

We all laugh a little, and then Craig ducks out toward the back of the house. He's claimed a corner room beside the back door for his home office. It looks like it might've been some kind of a parlor or dining room originally, as it's really big and has formal wallpaper. What's left of it, though—big surprise—is mostly faded and falling.

Annie leans back and sighs as she looks around, her bright blue eyes stretched wide like a child's at Disney World. "Imagine this. Me sitting in the Mantelle house with an actual Mantelle. You said at lunch you'd never been to Sophia Island before? Must've been a shock to see this place."

"Oh, it sure was. Craig had said it was big, but I had no idea. I think I glamorized living in an old home. This sure doesn't look like any of the magazines."

"So, your husband knew about the house? He's been here before? How is he related to Cora? There were always so many Mantelles to keep straight. A lot of them have moved away, but I bet the ones left here have enjoyed getting to see the house since they were forbidden from it for so long."

"There are Mantelles here? In Sophia Beach?" If so, this is the first I've heard of them. "Why were they forbidden from being in the house?"

"Oh, honey. There are more Mantelles

around here than you can shake a stick at. I'm surprised they're not coming out of the woodwork to get in here. As for why Cora forbade them from coming here, it was some old family fallout I reckon. Some of the old folks around might know. Then when Cora checked herself into the mental hospital, must've been almost ten years ago, she closed this place up good. Everybody always wondered what was going to happen to it."

I nearly choke on my sip of water. "Mental hospital? Why?"

Annie's eyes get even bigger, and she shrugs. "Probably was more like an Alzheimer's unit, who knows? But let's talk about this afternoon! What did Charlie say?"

"Charlie?"

"Charlie Greyson, Aiden's partner. Did he say who the dead man was?"

"No, but I talked to him apparently before lunch!" I wrap my arms around my waist again and try to warm up.

Annie nods. "That's what I heard. Are you cold, honey?"

I shrug. "I'm always cold, and this dark house doesn't help."

Annie picks up her glass of water and laughs. "It's 'cause you're so thin. Me? Now, I'm never cold. This heat here about burns me up. Love this time of year, though, 'cause it's still chilly."

I can't help but smile. At lunch every woman talked about how cold it's been. They were wearing coats, even some scarves. It's not hard to tell the tourists and recent arrivals from up north from the locals. We're the ones with our sleeves pushed up, no coats, wearing sandals in sixty-degree weather.

As Annie takes a drink, she jumps a bit. "Oh, there's my phone." She pulls it out of the pocket of her long jacket, answers it, then listens. Her eyes flash at me, and she says to the other person, "That's where I am now."

She presses the end button and lays the phone on the couch beside her while she takes a sip of water. "That was my youngest, Annabelle. She's manning my police scanner at the house. Something's going on with this thing. This wasn't just a heart attack or an accident like we thought."

While she was on the phone, I thought through our conversation. "You said you heard I'd talked to the man before lunch. Who did you hear it from?"

"Oh, everyone was talking about how the dead man was talking to a pretty lady in a red sweater and white pants on the dock. Guess the patrons at the restaurant saw him talk to you before he walked around to that big boat at the end. He had on a bright shirt, and it caught folks' attention. Wonder why he wasn't wearing that in the water?" She lifts her phone. "I'll text Aiden and tell him to check for that shirt."

"Oh, the police know. Well, they know that the man was wearing a Hawaiian shirt. I told them. Guess that's why it never connected when I saw the body. What is it?"

Annie's phone dings, and as she reads the text, her mouth falls open. Mouth still gaping, she looks up to stare at me, then whispers, "They've identified the body."

I lean forward. "Do you know him?"

She shakes her head, then shrugs. "Not exactly, but well, you might."

That makes me sit up straight. "Me? How would I know him? I just moved here! Besides, when I talked to him, I didn't know him. Who is—um, *was* it?"

Annie turns her phone toward me, and I stand up to get closer. One word jumps out at me, like it must've jumped out to Annie. *Mantelle*.

"Pierson Mantelle?" I murmur. "Who's that?"

Annie looks up at me. "He moved away years

ago. I kind of remember him from school, but like I said, there's too many Mantelles around here to shake a stick at."

Her phone dings again, and she lifts it. This time, her mouth settles into a thin line as she reads. "Yep. He was most definitely murdered."

"Murdered?" I squawk. Then I sink back onto the chair.

After another ding, Annie's mouth gets even tighter, and she types on her phone in a flurry. Then she practically throws it onto the little table near her. Well, the nearest one; there are several tables in the vicinity. "I'm just disgusted with myself. Here's a murder right under my nose, and do I stick around to investigate? No, I hurry home to listen to the police scanner. We could've been eating right there with the murderer, and I wasn't paying any more attention than a gnat!"

"But how do they know he was murdered?" I ask, ignoring the part about eating next to a murderer.

"He was hit on the head. Big glass margarita pitcher on the deck of his boat was lying there. Looks like someone grabbed hold of it and swung it at him. Well, that's what Adam says. Adam works for the marina. He's kind of the boss, so he was right there at the scene with the police until they discovered it wasn't just an accident." When her phone dings again, she leans over and reads it from its place on the table. "Adam again. Yeah, he says it's a mess down there at the marina. Yellow caution tape everywhere. Says you can practically hear the word 'murder' being passed from person to person."

I smile. "Adam? Let me guess: another one of your children?"

She grins and pushes off the couch to stand. "Yep. He's my oldest boy."

"How many children do you have?" I ask as I also stand.

"Six. Three boys, three girls."

"All of them have 'A' names?"

"Yep. Now, can I use your restroom?"

"Sure. Last room on the left past the staircase. Sorry that it's such a mess. All I've done is clean it a bit. I wasn't planning on having any company."

"Oh, it's fine. I won't be in there but for a minute, then I want to hear more about how you came to live here. If we're going to help Aiden and Charlie, I need to know more about the Mantelle family, don't you think?" She winks at me and heads down the hall.

I pick up my glass and carry it to the kitchen, saying to myself, "I think as a Mantelle, I need to know more about the Mantelle family. And for that, I think I'm going to need wine."

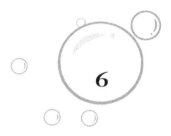

6

"Wait!" Annie puts her hand to her chest, bracelets rattling, and staggers back against the kitchen island where we were leaning to talk. "*Your* Craig is C. J. Mantelle, who spent summers here on Sophia? Now that I just didn't see at all. But *of course* it's him."

"C. J.? I don't know about that. I just know he stayed with his aunt Cora for the summers because his mother had to work. They lived in Atlanta." I sniff and shake my head. "C. J.? I've never heard anyone call my husband that." I look in Annie's direction, but all I can see is her mop of curls as she texts on her phone again. Probably to one of her kids.

I swirl the crisp pinot grigio around my glass. After Annie got out of the bathroom, I offered her some wine and we settled in to discuss what little I know about my in-laws.

It seems even Annie Bryant knows more than I do. She talks as she texts. "C. J. was a few years younger than me, but my sister and her friends would stalk him every summer when they were teenagers. His aunt Cora kept him pretty much to herself." She looks up at me. "I'm sure he told you all that, right?"

Her focus on me is intense, especially from someone who seems to be in a tizzy all the time. I shrug and turn to the sink. "Not really. We never talked about his summers here. He just said his aunt was crazy and pretty much a hermit."

We turn as Craig steps into the kitchen. "Who's a hermit?" he asks.

Over my shoulder I toss, "Your aunt."

He nods. "You're right about that. You can see from this house she was also a hoarder. Even before she checked into the care facility. What are we thinking for dinner? Can I get a glass of that wine?"

"Sure. So you finished your work?"

He nods as I hand him an empty glass.

Annie watches as he fills the glass from the bottle of wine still sitting on the counter. She takes a sip of hers, then says, "So you're C. J."

Craig lifts his glass. "I haven't been called that since the last time I was here, what, almost forty years ago." He tips his head, his dark eyes examining her with a smile. "Did we know each other then?"

Annie laughs. "No, but my sister and her friends stalked you around town and at the beach. You were always their summer mystery. I'm a few years older. Jewel says you didn't tell her about the other Mantelles in the area."

He shrugs. "Don't know anything about them to tell. I pretty much forgot about everything here when I went off to college. This isn't a place most of the world even seems to know about. My mother dumped me here with my crazy aunt every summer so she could work and not have to pay a sitter. Then she'd hurry back to Atlanta until the day before school started when she had to come get me."

I step closer to the kitchen island to screw the top back on the wine and put it in the refrigerator. "We found out who the man in the water was, honey. I guess it was one of your cousins— or second cousins? Pierson Mantelle."

"What?" he yells.

His exclamation surprises me, and I whirl around to look at him. However, he's moved away from us and is facing toward the windows.

"Craig? Did you know him?"

He takes a sip of wine, then turns back to face us. "Know him? I don't think so. Just hearing our last name, I guess, threw me off." He looks up at Annie. "Did you know him?"

Annie shakes her head and frowns. "Not really. He was quite a bit younger than all of us. In his forties, probably. His mom was the second wife and all that. I'm going to have to talk to some friends that keep track of all of that 'who is related to who' stuff. That is not my forte." She laughs, then looks down at her phone. "Uh-oh." She jerks her head up and looks at me. "Charlotte Bellington, you remember her from lunch today? Aiden and Charlie just left her house and are headed this way." She downs the rest of her wine in one gulp and then sits her glass on the old Formica. She leans on the counter with both hands. "Do you have a lawyer?"

Craig bursts out with a laugh. "A lawyer? Why would we have a lawyer? Jewel didn't see anything."

Annie focuses her intensity at him. "I'm serious. My Abbie is a lawyer, and I can get her over here in no time at all."

I tense and set my glass on the counter. "You think I need a lawyer?" When we hear a knocking at the front door, I grab Craig's arm. "Maybe we should get her daughter to come by?"

He sits his glass down beside mine and pats my back. "Let's just see what they want, okay?" He leaves the kitchen and goes to open the door. I follow him, but Annie hangs back in the kitchen.

"Mr. Mantelle, or should I call you C. J.? Why didn't you tell us earlier who you were? *C. J.*" Officer Greyson says as he comes in the door. This seems like a strange opening question to me, so I wait for Craig to respond.

"I haven't been called C. J. in decades. I wasn't hiding anything, just didn't think about it." He pauses and swallows. "How can we help you officers now?" Craig sounds wary, and the hair on my arms stands up.

Aiden smiles at me and tips his head. "Ma'am. My mother still here?"

"She was in the kitchen, but she may have left out the back door. She said she needed to go." Even as the words came out of my mouth I know Annie hasn't left but is still in the kitchen listening to our conversation. For some reason I'm glad about that.

Aiden calls out, "Mom?"

No one answers. Yep, Annie and I are on the same page.

Officer Greyson continues with Craig. "So did you know earlier that the deceased was Pierson Mantelle, your cousin?"

"How would I have known that? I didn't even know my cousin, if that's what he was. I don't remember any Pierson Mantelle from when I lived here. My family was a bit dysfunctional, I'm sure you know that. Besides, my mother never connected with her family after I was born. You can imagine getting to know my Mantelle cousins wasn't in my plans when we moved back here."

"Mrs. Mantelle." The officer turns to me. "Did you know Pierson Mantelle?"

"No, I, uh, no." I start to explain more but remember Annie's talk of a lawyer. And the hours of crime shows I've logged. Wrapping my arms around my waist, I look around for a jacket to put on. Either my northern blood has thinned in record time or the police are making me nervous because I'm suddenly freezing.

Craig sinks onto one of the ottomans near the front of the living room and sits with his elbows on his knees. "Wouldn't you know it? I come back to this place, and within a week some distant cousin gets himself murdered."

"What time did you get home today, Mr. Mantelle?" The officer nods at Aiden to take notes.

"I don't know. Around one? I left the job-site outside Daytona near ten. Made a couple detours to look at some things. Got lunch and came home. I really wasn't paying attention to the time."

"When and where were your last detour, sir? I need as clear of a timeline as I can."

Craig's mouth forms a thin line. "Bunnell Beach for gas. I think I stopped at a BP a little after eleven thirty and then came up through Jacksonville to look at a couple road projects my company's bidding on."

Aiden scribbles that down. I wait for Craig to ask why they want to know all that. I mean, *I* want to know why, but he just stares at them.

"Then you came straight home?" Greyson persists. "Went nowhere else in town?"

"No, straight home."

Greyson turns to me. "Ma'am, what time did you get home?"

"Two. Around that, I guess." I hold off a shiver. "Why? We didn't even know this man. We just moved here."

The officer clears his throat and makes a wrap-it-up motion to his partner as he steps back toward the front door. "Yes, ma'am, but you understand it seems a little fishy that your husband didn't tell us who he was when we were here earlier. It's not good when information comes out after the fact like that." At the door he puts his cap back on and turns to us. "So, there's nothing else either of you need to tell us, right?"

"No, nothing," I say, then look at Craig.

He shakes his head at me, then at the officers. Aiden tugs the big door open, tips his cap at me as he puts it on, and they both leave. When the door shuts, Craig pushes up on his knees to stand. "I think I'll go for a run." He heads to the main staircase that leads to the second floor and our bedroom.

I watch him climb the stairs; then, when he enters our bedroom and shuts the door, I tiptoe into the kitchen and whisper, "Annie?"

She peeks out of the butler's pantry, where she'd ducked behind boxes and bags stuffed with old vases and baskets. Our eyes meet, and we both sigh. She says, "Leaves me with one question."

"Me too," I say as I pick up our wine glasses and sit them in the sink. "How did Craig know his cousin was murdered?"

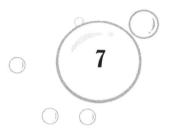

7

When I turn away from the sink, I look back at Annie, expecting to see her nodding in agreement. Instead her eyebrows are arched high and her mouth hangs open before she finally squawks.

"Oh my! That's right! How did he know Pierson was murdered, that it wasn't just a heart attack or something? Unless he was listening to us talk. Is that like him? To listen in on conversations?" Her bright eyes are wide as she grabs my arm. "Oh my, Jewel!"

I shake off her hand. I'm beginning to see Officer Greyson's reticence at having her involved. "No. Of course he doesn't listen in on conversations. Well, at least I don't think he would. But tell me what your one question is."

She takes a breath, and I can see her mind

backtracking. "Oh yeah. I wondered why the police were at Charlotte Bellington's, though I do believe your one question is better." She leans toward me and whispers, "Should we go ask him?"

"No, I'll ask him later. You're right. He probably just innocently overheard us, but he seemed surprised to hear who it was so he didn't hear us say that apparently. I'm sure it's nothing, but you're also right about Charlotte and the police."

Annie fluffs her curls and stands straighter. "Let's go see her."

I look around. I planned on getting so much done today, but our involvement in this mess really needs to be wrapped up. My nerves can't handle any more of the police popping in. "Okay, that's probably a good idea." We walk out of the kitchen, and at the bottom of the main staircase, which will be lovely once it's cleaned, then repaired—or is it repaired and then cleaned?—I yell up the stairs. "Craig, I'm going for a walk with Annie. Have a good run."

Annie is bent over at the front door, tugging on it with both hands as I walk up behind her. "Here, let me," I say. "You have to lift and pull." With the door opened and pulled shut again, we pause for a breath on the front porch. I find it pretty disorienting to have so much green in the yard in only March. What's crazy are all the falling leaves. Great bunches of them, just like an autumn day. The road is full of them, and they blow around in the wind.

Annie starts down the steps. "Charlotte's house is just a block this way, so let's walk." We pass through the driveway gate, which Craig and I always leave standing open, and turn right onto the sidewalk. Small patches of late afternoon sunshine provide a little warmth, but this is not so in the deep shade of the arching tree limbs and Spanish moss, where the chill is deep. My feet are cold, and I wish I'd changed out of my sandals.

"Do all six of your children live in the area?"

"Yes. Their daddy died when the oldest ones were in high school, so as soon as they graduated high school, they got jobs in the area or went to college around here before settling down. My Abbie, the lawyer, she went off for law school and talked about staying up in Georgia, but then wouldn't you know it, she fell in love with a man whose one great goal in life was living at the beach although he'd never even seen the ocean. And I'm not being cute about this being his *one* goal. She's as driven as they come, but…" She looks sideways at me and rolls her eyes. "He hangs out down at the beach and bartends, sometimes, and that's it."

I match her sigh with a shrug and add, "Sorry about your husband. That must've been hard."

"It was, but it was a long time ago. How many kids do you have? Where do they live?"

"We have four. Twin girls are the oldest, then two boys—not twins. Most of Craig's career we moved around the Midwest, and that's where they've all settled. Chicago and St. Louis for the girls, and both boys are in Wisconsin." I pause as my voice catches. "Long way from Florida."

She smiles and pats my upper arm, then waves her hand to my right. "Here we are."

The sign on the sidewalk reads "Bellington Manor Inn."

"Oh!" I exclaim. "I didn't even put the name together. This place is beautiful."

Annie holds an open hand up to me. "No. Do not mention the inn to Charlotte. Her daughter-in-law and son run it, and Charlotte hates everything about it. She pretends it doesn't exist." She points to the side of the property and straight ahead of us. As we continue for a few yards along the thick bushes and trees, there is a small path cutting off at an angle from the sidewalk. The path is obviously in the backyard of the inn, meandering away from the big house.

As we walk down it, the air grows stiller and darker as we head right into the low, thick limbs of the trees. The massive limbs swoop almost to the ground. The path ends at an adorable little house, like something out of a fairy tale. However, before I can ooh and ahh, Annie shushes me and shakes her head sternly. "No, none of that. She hates this, too."

Charlotte opens the door. "Thought I heard someone making their way through the woods," she says from inside the darkened doorway. "Good afternoon, Annie. Good afternoon, Mrs. Mantelle."

With a smile I step forward. "Please, call me Jewel."

She sniffs. "I hardly know you well enough for that sort of familiarity. I suppose you should come in before the bugs and mosquitos back in this swamp carry us all away. Annie, you can serve us tea. The water is ready. Mrs. Mantelle, welcome to my home."

She said 'home,' but her tone says she clearly meant 'cell.' "Thank you." I follow her inside and try not to appear interested in the adorable place. So clean and open, it feels more spacious than my huge home, which is stuffed with dark, dust, and junk. I'm free to look and enjoy since Annie is keeping up a loud stream of conversation all by herself from the kitchen. There's never a lapse in conversation with Annie around, I'm discovering.

Charlotte settles herself in a dusty-rose, high-backed chair. I sit in a chair across from her, with a back and seat cushion covered in the same dusty-rose silk fabric. A vase of cream roses scents the cool air, and it's hard to shake the fairy tale feel. Annie bustles in with the tea service. She sits down on the sofa with the empty table in front of it, which was obviously just waiting for tea to arrive.

"Charlotte, had you ever met this Pierson Mantelle?" Annie asks. "I've racked my brain but can't remember ever meeting him." She doesn't wait for an answer but continues jabbering on about town politics and gossip, which I know nothing about, as she pours hot tea into beautiful china cups. Seriously, it's hard to keep my swooning to myself.

Charlotte seems to settle even further into the cocoon of her tall chair once she has her cup of tea in hand. She answers Annie as she waits for it to cool. "Oh, I'm sure at some point I met Mr. Mantelle. The Bellingtons and Mantelles go back many years as founding families. Seems a shame for things to be so peaceful here on Sophia and then be disrupted by something

as horrific as murder. I blame so many new people moving in." After a daggered look at me, she
drops her focus to the rim of her cup, takes a sip,
then places her cup back in the saucer. She locks
her eyes back on me with laser focus, but speaks
to Annie. "I suppose you've brought her here to
find out what I told the police that sent them
back to her doorstep."

Annie laughs a bit. "Oh, is that what happened? I wasn't sure."

That got the Throned One's attention. She
slides her eyes to Annie, who looks so awkward
on the little couch. She's not only heavy, she's
tall. Big-boned. Her knees are as high as the
sweet little table in front of her, and the arm-
rests are way too low for her arms to rest on
them. But she smiles and sips; only her rapidly
blinking eyes give away that she is being visually
gored by the queen.

"Of course that's what you're doing here."
Charlotte swings her eyes back to me. "Tell me,
Mrs. Mantelle, why did you not tell us at lunch
exactly who your husband was? What are you
hiding?"

"Nothing. I didn't even know he was this C.
J. We never talked about his time here on Sophia Island."

She sniffs and stares at me. "So. He's a secret

keeper. Not enough of those left in my opinion."
She actually relaxes her shoulders as she continues. "All this talk about sharing everything and
communication in a relationship. Bah."

She lifts her cup and says, "I'll tell you what
I told the police because it is neither here nor
there to me. It's just a fact, and I believe in facts.
I saw a man on the docks while we were eating
lunch. He looked out of place. He also appeared
as if he wasn't sure what he was looking for. I'd
grown bored with the conversation and found
watching the man more interesting than hearing
another story about someone's *adorable* grandchild or dog." She takes another sip, rests her
cup back in its saucer, and then sets the saucer
on her side table.

Annie's eyes are turned down, like she's staring at her cup and saucer, which she has balanc-
ing on her knee. Her phone is buzzing away in
her pocket, but I don't believe she'll take it out
in front of Mrs. Bellington. Annie won't even
look up to meet my eyes. Why isn't she asking
Charlotte about this man? Finally, I break away
from looking at her and ask the question myself. "Why would the police be interested in this
man? What else did you see?"

Our hostess tilts her head to the side, away
from Annie, and she squints at me. "Tell me,

Mrs. Mantelle, what was your husband wearing today?"

I open my mouth, and it fills with the scent of roses and hot tea. The charming room suddenly feels too close. "He had on a white dress shirt and dark blue pants."

She smiles, and I honestly prefer her sneer. "Ah, well, that happens to be what the man I saw was wearing. Tell me, does your husband have dark hair with just a touch of gray? Is he in decent shape for his age, and does he have a dark, full beard?"

My chest lightens. "No—I mean yes, he has dark hair and is in good shape, but, no, he doesn't have a beard. Not even a mustache." I grin at her and bring my cup to my lips as she leans forward.

"Ah, this gentleman also didn't have a beard. He was clean-shaven." She leans back and smiles like the spider feeling the tug on her web. "Hmm, sounds very much like your husband *was* on the docks today. Headed to his cousin's boat, perhaps? His dead cousin's, that is."

When I look at Annie, she's pulled her phone out of her pocket and is reading it. She looks up at me and nods.

"Maybe I should go home," I mumble as I set my cup and saucer back on the tray. I put out my hand toward Annie when she starts to stand. "No, you stay. I'm fine by myself."

I never realized sand had a smell until we moved here. The sand I'm talking about is not the sand pushed around on the beach, cleaned by the tides and the ocean winds, but the gray sand that makes up the yards and driveways in the old part of town. This sand is old. Old and fine. As I look down, I grimace at the layer of gray on my feet and sandals. As a mom, and chief laundress in our home, I know about dirt from all around the country.

Black dirt from the Midwest agricultural areas that leaves dark, almost black stains on a toddler's pants. Red from the South, and from baseball diamonds, which makes red-orange rings on white socks and the knees of uniforms. Sand from the beach, which always came home from vacation with us by the buckets, but was very forgiving in the stain department.

This gray sand also doesn't leave stains; it's ghost dirt, so fine, so silky that it's not noticeable at first. Now I'm choking on it. I miss my kids, especially our first grandchild, Carver. In Illinois we didn't live in the same city as Carver and his parents, but it was less than an hour's drive. When I come to our black, iron fence I grab hold of it and look up. So many times through the years, Craig came in from work and told me where we'd be moving next. There were no discussions; it was part of his job. Like my brother in the military, we went where we were sent and asked no questions. When this move came up and retirement was an option, there was discussion, but looking back, I don't think it was that helpful. Being grandparents was so new that I don't think I even thought about what all we'd be missing. And what about the new baby our other daughter will be having at the end of the year? No, we didn't talk about missing the grandbabies.

I know I never thought of how odd or how different Florida would be. How much of a challenge this house would be. No, our discussion didn't include any of those things. Matter of fact, when any of the kids brought up any concerns, I laughed and brushed them aside. Can't worry the kids with my problems—not Sadie, who's a new mom, or Erin, who was correctly preoccupied with being newly pregnant and moving to a new town. The boys were always busy with college things and their own plans for the future. I would never saddle them with our concerns.

Letting my hand run along the black, iron bars, I walk toward our home. I remember the pastor who married us and his premarital counseling long ago. One warning he gave us seems to have finally come true: "Neither of you are talkers, and neither one of you likes confrontation. You both actively work to avoid conflict. You are going to have to force communication, I believe, or end up at a distance from each other."

Well, chalk one up for the preacher.

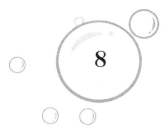

8

"Mrs. Mantelle?" The young lady standing in our front porch's shadows startles me as I approach our house. She steps out into the late afternoon sunshine. "I'm Abigale Bryant. My mom, Annie, sent me over."

She waits at the top of the steps. Her long, black hair hangs in a thick braid over one shoulder of her light blue skirt suit. She holds out her hand when I finally step up onto the top step. I'd taken my time, a bit stunned and not sure what to say. *Annie really thinks we need a lawyer?*

After a swallow I say, "I'm not sure we need a lawyer, Miss Bryant. Your mother may be jumping the gun." I shove open the door. "But I guess you can come in. I need to start supper."

The young woman follows me in, and her eyes dart around like everyone else's. She stops just inside the front door, both hands in front of her holding her shiny, new-looking briefcase. Both of our heads jerk toward the back of the house when we heard a door slam.

"Jewel?" Craig yells. "I'm home. Going to walk around the backyard for a minute with a Gatorade." I hold up a finger to the lawyer, then dash into the kitchen where my sweaty husband is closing the refrigerator while twisting the orange cap off his drink. "Oh, you are home," he says before he takes his first long drink.

I follow him out the back passage, past the butler's pantry, and toward the back door. "Craig," I demand to his back, although in a whisper. "Craig, we have to talk. Annie's daughter, the lawyer, is here. Were you at the marina today?"

He swallows as he pushes open the back door and jogs down the back steps into our own personal jungle.

"I'm trying to breathe here, Jewel. Give me a minute."

I also descend the few stairs but stop on the uneven brick patio and cross my arms, waiting for him to talk.

From behind us, Abigale says, "Here you are." She dashes down the steps. "Mr. Mantelle, come over here. Hurry!" She says all this in a stern whisper. "My mother isn't the only one that thinks you need a lawyer. My brother does, too. Aiden? I believe you met him and his partner, Officer Greyson, earlier today?"

"The policeman?" Craig asks.

She nods. "He gave me a heads-up that they are on their way back over here and *won't* be going back to the station alone."

Craig wipes his face with his hand and jerks around toward me. "Jewel? What's going on? You said you only saw the body!"

"Me? I'm not the one telling lies about where I was this afternoon. And it was *your* cousin that was murdered. By the way, how did you even know he was murdered? Were you eavesdropping on me and Annie?"

Abigale steps between us, waving her hand toward the front of the house. "Stop. A police car just pulled up. They're here. Don't say anything about anything, okay?" She prods me up the stairs, then opens the door at the top for me to walk through in front of her. She holds it open insistently until Craig walks back into the house. In single file we march to the front door. When Abigale reaches for it, I brush her off and try to work my magic. "Hello, officers."

"Mrs. Mantelle. Mr. Mantelle. Abigale." Officer Greyson looks over his shoulder at his partner. "Suppose your mother sent your sister scurrying over here?"

Aiden lowers his face and mumbles, "Suppose so."

Greyson steps toward Craig. "Mr. Mantelle. We need your fingerprints and to ask you a couple more questions."

"Why? It was my wife at the marina, not me."

"Craig!" I choke out, but once again, the lawyer interrupts.

"Hush, both of you. Is Mr. Mantelle under arrest?"

"We just need to verify the fingerprints on the scene are not his. That's all," Officer Greyson says. I start to breathe more easily, but then after a pause he adds, "For now."

Craig folds his arms across his chest, his eyes closed. Then they pop open. "Sure. I'll go with you. Why not? I've got nothing to hide, right? I wouldn't know anything about this if my wife hadn't come home talking about it all. Let me wash my face and change my shirt."

With that Craig turns and heads up the main staircase, taking the steps two at a time.

I lay my hand on Abigale's arm. "Will you go with him to the, to be fingerprinted? Should I go with him?" A knock at the door causes us all to look that way. "Excuse me," I say, as I weave between them and open the door.

There stands Annie with four of the ladies from lunch today. Officer Greyson groans, but Annie ignores him. The ladies swarm in, surrounding me.

"We're here to support our dear, dear friend," Annie explains in the midst of snippets of support from the other ladies. Snippets said while their necks nearly break from whiplash. They try to look at me, but how can I compete with *the* Mantelle house? "You go right on and take Mr. Mantelle down to the station," Annie continues. "Jewel will be just fine here with us."

Aiden and Abigale hiss at the same time, "Momma!"

Greyson folds his arms. "Miss Annie, exactly how in the world would you know where we're taking Mr. Mantelle?"

"Why, Officer Greyson, I assume that since our community has been rocked by this awful murder, you would be leaving not one stone unturned in exonerating the innocent. Right? You wouldn't be wasting valuable time on a wild goose chase, would you?"

Her blazing eyes are on level with the officer's, and he swallows as he takes a step back.

"No, ma'am. Just, just, oh, never mind." He turns and shouts, "Mr. Mantelle, let's go!"

Craig strides out of our bedroom and down the stairs. He brushes by us all, ignoring me, the women, even the officers, to stride out the door, which is still standing open. "I'm ready. Let's get this over so I can get back for dinner."

The officers and Abigale hurry after him. Abigale waves at her mother and gives me a wink as she pulls the door closed.

Annie takes charge. "Jewel, you remember Tamela and Cherry, who were with us at the marina when we saw the body."

I nod to Cherry, the tall, athletic nurse, and Tamela, the short teacher who had given Charlotte a ride.

"And then Lucy, who is our lunch group organizer."

"Oh, Jewel, I'm so sorry about all this, but we're going to fix it right up!" Lucy's blonde hair is styled perfectly. She's wearing a stiff khaki skirt and white golf shirt with Sophia Island's logo on the breast pocket. From the talk at lunch today, I recall she's on a lot of committees in town.

"Would you ladies like to sit down?" I ask.

Annie objects. "Oh no! We don't have time for that. I've been busy since I left Charlotte's."

Tamela, the retired teacher, steps forward

to lay a hand on my arm. "I couldn't believe it when Annie said she took you to Charlotte's. Oh my, she can be such a crotchety old woman! I consider carting her around my community service. Plus, she's my landlord, so staying on her good side is a good idea, even if it's darn near impossible."

"Enough of that right now, Tamela. We don't have long." Annie pauses and turns to me. "Now, Jewel, I know you don't know us that well, but we think we can help. You know. Help figure all this out. What did happen on the dock today?"

"But that's what the police are doing, right?" I shrug and take a deep breath. "Once they realize Craig wasn't on the docks and that his fingerprints don't match, we'll be out of the woods. I just want to forget this day ever happened."

"But honey," Tamela says as she squeezes my arm, "he *was* on the docks. I saw him."

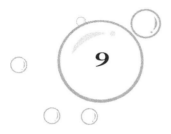

9

"No." I shake my head. "No. He wasn't down there. He came straight here. That's what he said."

Tamela sighs. "We hurried over here so I could get a look at your husband, and I'm sorry to say I did see him on the docks today. But that doesn't mean he's guilty of anything."

I sink onto the settee beside the staircase. "But why would he be down there? Why would he lie?"

Lucy sits beside me. "That's what we need to find out. First of all, however, I do know why Pierson Mantelle was here." At lunch I not only found out Lucy is a mover and shaker on Sophia; she's apparently an avid tennis player, and it shows in how controlled her actions are. Sitting on the edge of the couch, her knees are tucked together, the hem of her starched khaki skirt laying straight across them. Her arms are tanned, especially against the white of her shirt, and her short, blonde hair looks like she just came from the beauty shop, but I bet it always looks like this. She raises her hand and lowers her voice. "It's all rather hush-hush, but the city is looking at selling the marina. Pierson represented a group that was interested in buying it."

Annie pulls her phone from her pocket. "Girls, we have to go. Adam is waiting for us."

"C'mon, Jewel," Cherry says. She grabs my hand and pulls me up. "Five o'clock! It's Pirate Punch time!"

They bustle me through the door with them, everyone talking, but no one is answering my questions. Annie takes a break from leading our group to end up walking beside me. "Keep talking and thinking, ladies, I'll fill Jewel in." She leans down so I can hear her. "Adam is my son that works at the marina, remember? He's got the lowdown on Pierson Mantelle, so we're going to meet him at the Turtle Shell. Plus, it's happy hour, and their Pirate Punch is to die for."

The weathered wood of the two-story Turtle Shell sits along the railroad tracks to the port.

It frames a perfect view of the marina, the river, and the sunsets. Craig and I have already eaten here a couple times and watched the sun set on the water. Today, however, the ladies don't head for the outside area but ask the hostess for a table inside, pointing to one in the back corner.

"It is happy hour, right?" Cherry asks the hostess. The young woman smiles, nods, then asks, "Y'all want a round of the punch, Miss Annie?"

Annie grins. "Sure. How's your momma doing, Cherise? I saw her hobbling around on that scooter thing last week at the farmers market."

"Oh, Miss Annie, you know her. Can't get her to stop for nothing. I'll tell her you asked for her. That punch will be right out." When she approaches the bar, the young woman turns back toward us and yells, "Miss Annie, did you see Adam is up here at the bar? I'll tell him to come by and say hi."

As she darts into the kitchen to put in our order, the ladies all grin at each other. "That worked out better than we planned," Tamela whispers. "No need for us to accidentally bump into him now. Everyone in the place heard that."

Annie shimmies her shoulders and beams. "I just knew we'd be really good at this detective stuff."

Okay, they seem to be enjoying this just a little too much. This already doesn't feel real, and they are not helping me get my feet on solid ground.

Lucy gets up and talks to some of the other diners in the restaurant while Annie and Tamela go to the restroom. That leaves me and Cherry alone at the table for a few minutes. She scoots over to sit beside me. "You look a bit stunned, honey. You okay?"

"I am stunned. What in the world am I doing here when my husband is talking to the police? I know Tamela says she saw him on the dock, but that can't be right. He wouldn't just lie."

"Maybe he didn't think it was important earlier. All I know is these ladies here know everything there is to know about Sophia Island, so I'd let them help. It's a nice-sized town with a lot of tourists. The paper mills bring in a lot of folks, too, but all in all it's just another Southern small town." Her head lifts as our table mates and the waitress with her tray of pink drinks head our way. Out of the side of her mouth Cherry says, "Let them help you and your husband. I don't think they can truly hurt anything." She slides back into her seat.

"Look who I found over at the bar," Annie announces. "Adam, meet Sophia Island's newest resident, Jewel Mantelle. Jewel, this is my oldest son, Adam. He was just having a beer at the bar, and I told him to join us for a minute. Is that okay with you ladies?"

Having completed her performance, Annie retakes her seat beside me, making room for Adam on her other side. Lucy switches seats with Cherry to sit next to Adam, saying something about an air vent blowing on her hair. They are talking too loudly. Their eyes as they look at each other are too big and too full of meaning. They are just being—too everything.

I'm not so sure I agree with Cherry's thought that they can't hurt anything.

"Nice to meet you, Mrs. Mantelle," Adam says. He reminds me of my son Chris, although Chris seems to be a few years younger. They both look like serious young men who like being outdoors.

"Hello, Adam." My mouth is so dry that I reach for my pink drink in its plastic cup and take a long pull from my straw. "Whoa, that's really good," I manage to get out before I start coughing. And laughing. Along with everyone else at the table.

"Pirate Punch definitely has a punch," Annie says. "You might better sip at it." She folds her arms on the table and sinks down a bit. She twirls her finger at Cherry and Tamela, and they immediately start talking to each other, rather loudly, about some movie they'd recently seen.

Annie then whispers, "Now, son, what is going on? Why was Pierson Mantelle here on Sophia?"

Adam leans forward on his folded arms, too. "He was holding some meetings on his boat. Actually had Colby's bring out food and containers of margaritas."

I whisper, "Like the one he was hit with?"

"No, these were plastic jugs, almost like milk jugs. They use them to deliver drinks to boats. The one he was hit with was one of those big, heavy pitchers they have in Mexican restaurants." He holds his hands out in a wide circle. "Big, thick glass, with a blue rim. He had glasses that matched, so I think the whole set was from his boat."

I take a sip of my drink, then with my hand still on my straw, I ask, "Did you see my husband on the docks?"

Adam looks down, then at his mother, then at me. "I don't know. I only saw a man with long sleeves on, a dress shirt. His head was in the shadows. I was helping the boat owner in the next slip, and as I walked by, I glanced onto the Mantelle boat. The only other thing is that there were some women on the boat. Y'all should be able to find out who from somebody at Colby's, since they were taking food to the boat."

Lucy leans in closer. "Has Pierson been here on his boat often? Where's he from?"

Adam shrugs, then nods. "Occasionally. But, like, he never gets off it much that I know of. He has food delivered sometimes and walks around the docks a bit. He never stays more than one night."

Lucy writes a note on her napkin. "Let's find out where his boat is registered. I have no idea where he lives now." She grimaces and corrects herself. "Lived, I suppose."

Adam sighs and drops his head even lower. "Who would've ever imagined a murder at the marina? Two hurricanes back to back and now this? It's like we're cursed. All of us at the marina are pretty nervous about what's going to happen. If I get laid off, I might have to leave Sophia and really don't want to do that, but… " He shrugs again, then sits back and finishes his beer. "I need to get home. Mom, the kids will want to know if you're going to dinner at church tonight."

"Not tonight. We have too much to do with our case." As her son stands up, she says, "Tell the kiddos I'll come over tomorrow. Give Leesa a break."

He bends down to hug her, then moves around behind her. "Good luck, Mrs. Mantelle. It was nice to meet you."

"You, too, Adam." Then I lower my voice. "Thanks."

The crowd in the restaurant has grown while we've been talking. As I look around, Lucy and Annie are whispering to my side. Cherry and Tamela are still discussing movies, although I get the feeling they're making up stuff to say at this point. Annie motions for me to lean closer.

"Lucy says Pierson had been talking to, and maybe working with, some of the councilmembers on selling the marina. Can you believe that?"

Cherry leans toward us. "I know I've only lived here five years and we don't own a boat, so all I ever do at the marina is watch the sunset, but how can someone just buy a marina? And how can a city just sell one?"

Lucy picks up her drink, but before putting the straw in her mouth, she says, "That's what a lot of folks want to know." She opines with raised eyebrows, "Not a lot of answers around here lately."

Annie's phone buzzes. She reads it, then

looks at me. "Aiden says he's taking your husband home in about five minutes."

Cherry toasts me with her punch. "Well, that's good news. They didn't arrest him."

"Of course they didn't arrest him," I say with a small laugh, but with a sinking stomach, I realize I should have been worried about that. I stand up. "I need to go home. Be there when Craig gets there. I'm sure he's got everything figured out. How much do I owe?"

All four ladies shake their heads at me. "We've got it," Annie says. "You just go on home."

I push my chair in and thank them all. "I really appreciate it, ladies. Hope you solve the mystery. I'm just glad Craig is out of it. They wouldn't have let him leave if he wasn't, right?" They all smile and give me the thumbs-up. As I head toward the front door, I decide I should stop in the restroom before walking home. When I abruptly turn, I see all those smiles and lifted thumbs at the table have turned to frowns and shaking heads.

Never mind the restroom. I need to get home.

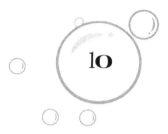

10

When I walk through our open gate, there's a woman coming around the corner of our house.

"Can I help you?" I ask. I can't believe that we've had no company in the last month, but now someone's waiting for me every time I return.

The woman looks about my age, maybe older, though I'm not that good at guessing ages. She's wearing a black jersey dress with three-quarter sleeves; big, dark sunglasses; and black wedge sandals. Her black hair is pulled back into a ponytail that swishes as she walks toward me. I've noticed people in Florida wear sunglasses even when the sun is going down. I'm not sure what that's about.

As we reach each other she holds out her hand. Our hands meet, and she says, "Hello,

Mrs. Mantelle? I'm Leigh Anne." She places her free hand over our entwined hands and presses. "Leigh Anne Mantelle."

"Oh! Oh, so you're related to my husband. I've not met any of the family, but I'd heard there were quite a few of you around. I'm Jewel. Won't you come in?" I pull my hand away from hers and hold my other hand out toward the front steps.

"I'd love to." She strides up the stairs, then waits for me. When I shove in the door with my hip, I notice I'm getting a little sore on that hip. I rub it as she rushes past me.

"My, it's quite full, isn't it?" She turns to me as she whips off her sunglasses. Only her hands tell her age, as her face and neck are quite smooth. I believe she's had some surgical help, but I'm not good at spotting that either. Her eyes, a fabulous moss green, stare at me and hold my attention. I really do have to start using face cream more religiously. She breaks her gaze to look around again; then she sighs. "I haven't been in here in, oh, probably decades. Cora sure took being a hermit to heart with all this junk."

"Yes. Yes, it is quite full. No idea if any of it is good enough to keep. Do you live near here?"

She laughs as she folds her sunglasses and

tucks them into a little black purse. "Oh my word! No, not at all. We live in Ponte Vedra."

She says that like I should know that living in Ponte Vedra means something. People do that when you move to a new place, assume you make all the correct assumptions based only on their well-enunciated words. So I ignore it. Then I remember the dead man, Pierson Mantelle. "Oh, did you hear? I mean about what happened with that Mr. Mantelle at the marina?"

She draws in a breath but before she can speak, her eyes go distant and she collapses onto the settee behind her. Luckily, it would be hard to collapse in this packed room and hit the floor.

"Oh no! Mrs. Mantelle? Leigh Anne, are you okay? Let me get you some water."

I rush off to get a bottle of water, and as I come back with it, the front door flies open. Craig bellows, "They told me to not leave—" He stops when he follows my eyes to our company.

"Craig, this is Leigh Anne Mantelle."

The woman gathers herself and sits up a little straighter, then holds out her manicured hand. Craig hesitates with another quick glance at me before walking over and taking her hand for just a moment.

"Hello," she says, staring into his face. "I believe we are cousins by marriage."

Craig shrugs a bit and lifts his hand at the water I've just given her. "Think I'll get something to drink, too." He walks out of the room.

I sit down, a little off guard at how short Craig acted, but then again, he did just come from the police station. I wait while Leigh Anne takes a long drink.

"Thank you. I needed that." She looks toward the kitchen, obviously waiting for Craig to return, so I wait, too. When he comes back with a tumbler of some sort of brown liquor on ice, he sits across the room from us on a formal side chair.

Our guest tilts her head up gently in a questioning mode. "So you were at the police station?"

Craig's head snaps toward me, and he glares. I squawk, "I didn't say that!" I look at her. "I didn't tell you that."

She softly laughs. "Why would I need you to tell me anything? I was born here. I know more about what's going on in Sophia Island than you'll ever know." She looks back at Craig, and her voice takes on a hard edge as she says, "Isn't that right, C. J.?"

He shifts in his chair and downs the rest of his drink.

She suddenly stands and, with her hands on her slim hips, declares, "Honestly, every time I come back here, I remember why we moved away. It's such a tacky little town, don't you think? Pirates? Turtle Shells? Honestly." She flutters her hand in dismissal as she stalks toward the front door, slowly examining everything around her. "And you being saddled with this, this *house*. Poor things."

Neither Craig nor I move. All our energy has drained out of us. There is nothing at all left to make us stand, say goodbye, or even care that Leigh Anne is leaving. It's like I'm watching her on the television, and all that's left to do is to turn it off.

She turns to face us as she pulls out her sunglasses, unfolds them, and places them on her face. She continues with her over-the-top soliloquy. "Only something dreadfully important could make me come back to my godforsaken hometown. Only something like the murder of my son."

My mouth drops open, and Craig springs from his chair. Leigh Anne flips around, ponytail flying out, and opens the front door. She's gone before Craig gets to the edge of the old carpet. Before I even stand up.

I join Craig on the porch, and we watch her stalk down the sidewalk, through the gate, and get into the low-slung car she'd parked on the street.

As she roars off, lethargy settles back over me. I sink onto a window ledge beside the door. "This is a mess. What did the police say?"

"Not to leave town." He looks around at me. "I'm starving. What is there to eat?"

I lean over my knees and hug my legs. I don't want to eat. I lift my head and force out the question. "Were you on the docks this afternoon? Did you go to Pierson Mantelle's boat?"

He pushes his hands into the pockets of his khaki pants and jingles his car keys. He's already jogging down the front steps when he says, "We'll talk when I get back with some dinner."

I watch him leave just as I watched Mrs. Mantelle leave.

I don't know what to think about either one of them right now.

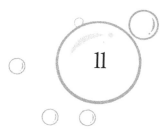

11

"I put your salad in the fridge. You'd already gone up to bed when I got back last night," Craig says to me as I creep down the long staircase the next morning. At his voice, I straighten up, tighten the belt on my robe, and walk faster. I'm still mad.

"So you're home. You know, I probably wasn't asleep when you got home, even though it took you *hours* to find some dinner. You could've come upstairs."

He leans back on the couch as he sips his coffee. "I was fine down here."

I sit on the chair next to his end of the couch. Blankets and pillows are piled on the other end, where he spent the night. My anger seeps away, and I can't hide the sadness in my voice. "I thought we weren't going to start this here? You sleeping on the couch or in the guest room."

He shrugs, not even looking at me, so I get up and make myself a cup of coffee. From the kitchen I say, "So you didn't tell me about the police station."

"Listen, it's not a big deal…" His voice drags off, and then he's quiet. When I come back into the living room, he's scooted up to the edge of the couch and turned toward the chair I was in, his elbows planted on his knees. Craig is a runner, but his build doesn't look like a runner's. He's square, and his legs are short. He looks more like a wrestler. Anyway, he's attractive and healthy-looking. His dark hair has only a few gray strands in it, and his smile can light up a room. We've not had much to smile about lately, though. My coffee cup on the side table, I sit in the chair and show I'm listening.

Just like our counselor said to do.

He takes a deep breath and repeats, "It's not a big deal, but I *was* at the marina yesterday."

"Craig! You said—"

His sharp look reminds me to not interrupt, so I stop talking and lift my cup to my lips.

"I know I said I wasn't there, but I was embarrassed, I guess. Like I told the police, you said you were going to Colby's for lunch, so I went down there to find you and maybe talk you into having lunch with, with me." He sounds unsure, embarrassed, unfinished. Avoiding my eyes, he gets up and walks toward the side window, where he pulls open the curtain, but between the dirty window and the bushes pressed against the house, there is nothing for him to look at. I stay perfectly still so he can finish. With a sigh, he drops the curtain back in place before turning back to me with a smile. "But I didn't see you, so I came on home."

Letting a pause happen to show I heard what he said and am thinking about it, I take another sip of coffee. I follow it with another deep breath before I ask, "Did you see Pierson Mantelle?"

He clenches his jaw but quickly releases it, covering any anger or impatience with another smile. "I might as well tell you, since the police know. Pierson had emailed me. I knew the police would be going through his email, so I wanted to come clean with them."

"You knew him? The man who, uh… You'd been talking to him? But I thought you didn't know any of your relatives here."

"I didn't know him. He got my information from the real estate agent and wanted to know my plans for the house. My aunt Cora had cut herself off from the family years ago, but I get the feeling they all thought they'd get a share in her estate." He scoffs. "Everyone but me. You know I never even thought about this place. These people. I guess they were all as surprised that I inherited everything as we were. I think it was my aunt's last chance to stick it to them all, but she wanted it to stay in the family, so…" He looks around us, then meets my eyes. "I knew I should've refused it. I was right, wasn't I?" He doesn't wait for me to answer as he holds up his empty coffee cup. "I'm getting another cup, and then I need to get to work. This really hurts me not being able to be onsite. Maybe they'll get this mess cleared up today." He walks into the kitchen, leaving me wondering if I'm really that bad at listening or if he didn't actually say anything.

I follow him into the kitchen and lean against the island across from him. He's facing the single-serve coffeemaker, watching it fill his cup. "So did you see Pierson Mantelle?" I ask.

As the coffeemaker finishes with extra sound and fury, my husband doesn't move or speak. When he does, he lifts his cup as he shakes his head at me. "I need to get to work." He walks out the back door of the kitchen to his office and firmly shuts his door behind him.

I just as firmly open it up and step inside. "We weren't through talking."

His surprise as he looks up from where he's bent over his desk almost makes me smile. I hold it back. "Why was he emailing you? Did you go see him? I deserve some answers. I tried listening to you, but you didn't say anything." I don't want to be confrontational, so maybe if my body language is relaxed it'll help. I lean on a stack of boxes beside the door and uncross my arms. And smile, or at least try to.

He takes a deep breath and licks his lips. "Okay. Like I said, he wanted to know my plans for the house. I emailed him back that we were keeping it. He wanted to talk about that. That's it."

"So did you talk to him? Did you see him yesterday?"

He slowly stands, walks over to me, and stands close. With me leaning on the boxes, he's taller than me, so I stay relaxed, looking up at him. Letting him be taller. Listening.

"I came to the marina looking for you to see if you wanted to have lunch. I didn't see you, so I came home. Now, I have a conference call in ten minutes and some work to do before that, so if you can hold the rest of your questions until later, I would appreciate it." He rubs my upper arm, then turns back to his desk.

As I walk out, his office door is once again firmly shut.

Instead of heading back to the kitchen I turn to my left and open the back door. The morning air feels not hot, but heavy. I can only imagine how much thicker it will be when it's actually summer. It's only March now. While we've lived in a lot of places, the farthest south was Tennessee for a year, and I thought that was too hot. Why in the world I jumped on moving to Florida is beyond me...

Oh yeah.

I was trying to save my marriage.

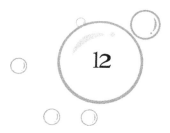

12

"Cute pajamas," Annie says when I pull open our front door. This is quickly followed by, "Get dressed. I'll just get a cup of coffee while you do." She bustles through the front door, past me, and right into the kitchen.

I fold my arms around my waist; feeling the soft fabric makes me smile. My cotton pajamas have pink ballerinas on them. I bought three sets of them last Christmas, one for each of my grown daughters and me. They have button-up tops and long pants, and I couldn't resist them because they reminded me of the matching pajamas the girls wore when they were little.

I follow her. "Dressed for what?"

"Oh Lord, my Abbie has one of these contraptions. These pod things... There, I think that's right. We're meeting Lucy for coffee downtown. She's got the lowdown on the marina being sold. Go get dressed," Annie scolds as she turns to look at me. "I'd've called you, but I realized in all the excitement yesterday I forgot to get your phone number."

I'm halfway up the stairs when she yells, "Dress nice. We might have to go to town hall. Oh hey, Mr. Mantelle. You working from home today?"

Let her and Craig work it out, I think as I dash into our bedroom and quietly shut the door.

I pull on a tunic dress of lightweight turquoise fabric and slip on a pair of gold sandals. Clipping my hair back with a gold clasp, I look in the mirror and sigh. One thing I've noticed about the women here is that they tend to wear makeup every day. Even worse? It looks good. Yesterday at lunch I noticed the lipsticks and thick lashes on the women my age and older and wished I'd learned to do all that better. I pull open my makeup drawer, find a lipstick I probably bought for one of my kids' high school graduations, and try it on. I start to wipe it off, then imagine my daughter Erin saying, "Leave it, Mom. You've got to get used to it." My other daughter, Sadie, would shrug and say, "Whatever, Mom. Let's go." They are twins only because they were born at the same time.

"Okay," I say into the mirror as I drop the tube of lipstick into my pocket and straighten up. "I'll try it." I shut the drawer and leave the bathroom before I can change my mind.

"You're as cute as a bug's ear!" Annie says from the living room as I come down the stairs. "I love them tunic dresses, but I can't wear them straight things with my big ol' boobs. If I bend over in something like that, you can see everything I got." She struggles off the low couch and sets her coffee cup in the kitchen while I collect my purse. "I'll wait for you on the front porch."

She's still fighting with the front door by the time I get ready to go.

"Here, let me." I push, lift, and pull to get the door to swing open, and we step out.

Once I close the door she says in a quiet voice, but with lifted eyebrows, "So, your hubby is working from home today? He didn't seem real fond of finding me in your kitchen."

"He's not in a good mood. I guess the police told him not to leave town. At least I think he said that. What did Aiden say about what happened at the police station yesterday?"

We walk down the sidewalk toward her car.

"He was busy last night so we didn't get to talk, but he did talk to his girlfriend. She works at the coffee shop I told Lucy to meet us at. Can

you believe her name is Eden? Aiden and Eden."
Annie rolls her eyes. "And wouldn't you know,
he seems serious about this one."

We drive through the morning shadows on
the old streets, and she pulls into a small parking
lot marked with several No Parking signs.

"Should we park here?" I ask.

"Yeah, it's my daughter Amber's building.
Comes in handy always having a parking spot
since I don't live downtown."

"What kind of business is your daughter in?"

"Real estate. She's put every cent she's ever
earned into property, and it's paid off for her."

We walk out of the little gravel lot and down
the sidewalk toward Centre Street. Crossing the
main street and turning right on the sidewalk,
the charm of Sophia Island is thick. The sky is
a clear morning blue, and there's a breeze rus-
tling the palm trees. Leafy bushes in the corner
planters ruffle as the wind passes through them.
Most of the shops are still closed, so the sidewalks are empty except for a few people walking
their dogs. On the next block, however, there
are people seated at little tables and benches
outside Coffee Sophia, a small place tucked between shops, art galleries, and restaurants.

Annie talks to several people as we walk
through them and find a place in line. She looks

around, especially behind the counter. "There's Eden. Eden!" she shouts as she waves. She makes several cryptic motions with her hands, ending by shouting, "Thank you!" Whispering, she says, "She's getting us a table. I texted her that I'd need one with at least three chairs."

"So is that a service for anyone, or just for someone related to her boyfriend?"

Annie furrows her brow and frowns. "I don't know. Never thought about it." She brightens. "There's Lucy." We wave as the man behind the counter speaks up.

"Your usual latte, Mrs. Bryant?"

"Yes, but instead of vanilla, give me raspberry. That sounds more like spring, don't you think?"

He nods, then looks at me. "And you, ma'am?"

I grimace at how everyone calls me 'ma'am' down here. It makes me feel so old. "I'll take a regular coffee, and I'll add my own cream and sugar. Also, you don't have to call me ma'am," I add with a big smile.

Annie laughs. "Oh, he does too have to call you ma'am, or his momma will be over here kicking his behind. Isn't that right, Michael?"

"Yes, ma'am, it is!" he says with a wink before turning his attention to the next person in line.

We find ourselves being directed to the rear of the shop where Eden waits beside a small table. "Hey, Mrs. Bryant. I got you and your friends a table," the young woman says. She's slight and has tattoos on all of her exposed skin—which is a lot. Her red hair is short and cut choppily so that it sticks out.

Annie gives her a big hug, then holds her at arm's length, staring in her face. "Tell me something, Eden. Do you get tables like this for everyone or just for me because you're dating Aiden?"

"Oh." The girl's face scrunches in concern, and the flower tattoo on her cheek turns an appealing pink. "You always text to let me know you're coming, so I just, well, I mean, you are Aiden's mother."

Annie hugs her again. "Oh, you are a sweetie." She turns Eden toward me. "This is my new friend, Jewel Mantelle." At Eden's widened eyes she adds, "Yes, Mantelle like the house. She's the one living there! Eden loves antiques and loves the old houses."

"Yes, ma'am, I sure do. I really love your house. Can't believe you get to live there!" She squeals and then jumps when someone shouts her name. "I've got to get to work, but here." She pulls a folded-up piece of paper out of her jean pocket and gives it to Annie. "Here's what I got from Aiden this morning." As she ducks away from us, she whispers back, "Can't believe there was a murder right here on Sophia!"

We sit down, and Annie shakes her head. "Isn't she the sweetest? Those tattoos are something else, but then, it is the family business. Now let's see what she got from Aiden."

She spreads the paper out on the table, but from my angle I can't make out the messy writing. I sit back, take my phone out of my purse, and look at it. There are two texts from Erin, the one of my four children who checks in every day. It's strange how kids raised in the same family can have such varied opinions on communicating with their parents. There's nothing from the other three. When all this gets straightened out, maybe I'll fill Erin in, but right now what would I even tell her? I turn off the screen and lay it on the table just as Lucy comes up.

"Good morning, ladies. What's that you're studying, Annie?"

"Notes Eden got from Aiden about our case. They did find that Hawaiian shirt Pierson had had on earlier on the boat, so no doubt he was the same man Jewel talked to. The big glass pitcher was the murder weapon; no prints on it, so it must've been wiped clean. It had had margarita in it from Colby's. Pierson's girlfriend and one of her friends were on the boat, but his wife was not." Annie looks up from the paper to meet our eyes with her eyebrows raised.

"Seems they hadn't been able to talk to his wife as of yesterday. They live in Ponte Vedra," she says.

"Oh," I interject. "That's where his mother lives, too. She came to see us yesterday."

At the same time, Lucy and Annie exclaim, "Leigh Anne Potts?" They look around to see if anyone is paying attention to them, but the loud coffee shop covers their noise.

I lean toward them. "Well, she said she was Leigh Anne Mantelle. She didn't tell us Pierson was her son until she was leaving."

"Potts was her maiden name," Lucy says. "When I see her at tennis matches, it's all I can do to remember she's a Mantelle." She sniffs. "I try to not remember her at all, but I guess that's mean, seeing as her son was killed yesterday. Wonder where she's staying."

Annie lays down the sheet of paper. "You don't think she's staying with her mother, do you?"

"I think if she could get out of it she wouldn't even stop in and say hello to her mother. I bet she's at the Isle." Lucy pulls out her phone and punches in a number while Annie goes back to deciphering Eden's handwriting.

Our drinks are delivered, mine with a small pewter container of cream and a matching bowl of sugar. None of the other tables have them, and I wonder if they are another perk of being here with Annie. I had thought I'd take my cup over to the fixing station, but this is really nice, knowing people.

"She isn't at the Isle, according to Davis," Lucy says. "Davis is my, well, my friend, and he is one of the owners of the resort."

Annie grins. "He's a very good friend. A very good, rich, handsome friend, right?" She punctuates her description with some elbow nudges.

Lucy shrugs and points at the paper. "What else does that say? I have things to tell y'all, too. I'll track down Leigh Anne Potts later."

Annie goes back to reading out loud. "The girlfriend and her friend both claim they were on the back of the boat, tanning and possibly asleep. They knew people came and went on the boat, but they didn't pay any attention. They apparently only became alarmed when they couldn't find any more margaritas." She reads further, then drops the paper and rolls her eyes. "Both women are only twenty and were less concerned with Pierson dying than with how they'd get back to school. Apparently they go to college in St. Augustine."

Lucy and I both wrinkle our noses. "Ew, twenty?" I ask. "That's disgusting."

Eden comes up to the table. "Let me guess, you got to the part about the girlfriend? I forgot to write down that Aiden said the thought is that they were too drunk to even lift up the pitcher. Apparently it was heavy, even when empty." She sets a plate on our table. "Here's some of the crumb cake edge pieces for y'all to share. Can I get you anything else?"

Though we all say no, she lingers. She bends down to whisper and point to the piece of paper. "Just be sure to not let Aiden know I gave you that, okay?" She looks like a guilty child with her big eyes roaming around the table to meet each of ours.

Lucy and I smile and shake our heads at her. Annie grabs her arm. "Of course not, you sweet thing. You know if I'd talked to Aiden he would've told me all this himself, but I really didn't want to infringe on the short time he gets to spend with you."

Eden tries to smile, but mostly just nods as she backs away.

"Really?" I ask. "Your son would tell you all

this? My sons barely even answer my texts." I hope I kept the self-pity out of my voice.

Annie plops her folded arms on the table and stares at me. "Are you kidding? I may cross all kinds of boundaries with my kids, but this kind of information only comes from pillow talk." One side of her mouth crooks up into a grin. "Cultivating as a source the girl sharing my police officer son's pillow, however, that's a boundary I'm more than willing to ignore."

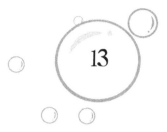

13

Out on the sidewalk, traffic has picked up, both walking and driving. Lucy darts through the outside tables, keeping her eyes up. Annie laughs as we try to follow her.

Annie pushes me along, saying in my ear, "Lucy knows she'll get stopped to talk if she hesitates even a bit. She's a born politician, knows how to talk to *every*body. Or *no*body. And not tick off *any*body!"

When we catch up to her, Annie grabs Lucy's arm. "Slow down there, mama. We're safe here." She pulls us into the alcove of a closed business. "Now tell us what you found out."

The petite blonde rolls her eyes and straightens her short navy jacket. She's wearing it over a tailored, blue-and-white striped linen dress. Even after sitting for the last half hour, she still looks pressed as a leaf in a middle school science notebook. Her artful swoops of short hair make me think again of cutting mine off, but I know mine hangs limp and straight whether it's three or thirty inches long. At least with a little length I don't look like a wannabe British pop star.

Lucy rolls her eyes. "Sorry for all those interruptions while we were trying to talk in there. Everyone seems to think I know what's going on in town."

Annie leans against the old brick wall. "Because you do. And you love it, so tell us what you know before the inquiring minds find you."

"Okay. Pierson Mantelle and one of the councilmembers, Ray Barnette, have been in talks for a while about the city selling the marina to a private company. Pierson represented the private company, but it wasn't exactly his company like I thought. He was brought in because of his ties to Sophia."

Annie scrunches up her face. "Ties to Sophia? He's not lived here in twenty years. Maybe more." Her eyes slide to me. "But look at C. J. He's not lived here in close to forty years—even then it was only for summers—and now he's owner of one of the oldest mansions on the island. So who knows?"

I speak up. "And didn't you say Pierson's mother is from here, too? Is his dad still alive?"

Both women nod at me. "He's quite a bit older than Leigh Anne. He had a stroke a few years ago. Last I heard was in a nursing home in Jacksonville, but he is still alive," Lucy says. "Edison Mantelle was already in his forties when he met Leigh Anne, and she was only right out of high school."

Annie huffs. "Apple doesn't fall far from the tree, does it?"

Lucy agrees. "I called my aunt who remembers all the gossip. Leigh Anne came home after her first semester at Florida State and caught Edison Mantelle's eye. He was married, but well, you know how that goes. Aunt Jean said he'd already made a bunch of money and spent a lot of time all over the state. He set up Leigh Anne in Ponte Vedra where she was his mistress until she got pregnant that next summer. Then he got a quick divorce and married her. Really set off his wife and their kids. He left them here, high and dry as possible."

"Oh my word! I hadn't put all that together," Annie says. "Sue Martin took back her maiden name and moved to the north end of the island. I'd completely forgot she was married to Pierson's daddy. She remarried, didn't she? And that makes—what were her kids' names? They were just a few years younger than me."

"Cora and Howard. Remember? They named them after the original owners of the house," Lucy says as she arches an eyebrow at me.

"My house?"

"Yes," she says. "Surely you've read the historical marker out in front of it. Those two might harbor some ill feelings about their younger sibling, who was given everything their father took with him to Ponte Vedra. We should look into them." She checks her watch. "I have to go, but let's walk toward the courthouse. Anyway, Pierson and Barnette did meet yesterday on his boat. That could help clear your husband, Jewel. Since Barnette could've been wearing a dress shirt, he might have been the man that Adam saw."

We walk down the sidewalk in a huddle, with both Annie and me bent over Lucy to hear her. After crossing the street a couple of blocks west, we stop at the fountain in front of the courthouse. Lucy turns and looks up at us. "I made you an appointment with Ray Barnette. I used your name, Jewel. I figured the Mantelle name would open doors, and it did. He's waiting for you up on the second floor."

I look up at the old windows in the elaborate

building. "So the council members have offices in the courthouse?"

Lucy pats me on the back. "Not exactly. Ray, um, works here sometimes."

Shielding my eyes from the sun, I look more closely at Lucy to see her grinning. "What's so funny?"

"Nothing. Go find out what you can from Ray. I'll walk you in, I need to have a word with one of the judges on the first floor—not anything to do with our case. Then I have a board meeting at the chamber to rush to." She steps forward as Annie sits down on the brick edge of the fountain.

"What are you doing?" I ask Annie. "We're going inside."

"No, I really can't." She pulls her phone out of her pants pocket and starts playing with it, ignoring Lucy and me.

"Why not? I don't know what to ask. I thought you wanted to be a detective."

"Oh, I do." She looks at me and nods. "But I can't go talk to Ray with you. You'll be fine." She looks back down at her phone. "I'll do some research on Pierson's stepsiblings."

Lucy tucks her arm around one of mine and pulls me to the front doors. "Honestly, Jewel, it'll be better like this. You see, sweetie, Ray and Annie kind of date sometimes."

She pulls open the ornate doors, and we enter a quiet, dark hall.

"And," she says with a sigh, "apparently this isn't a sometime."

At the top of the wide, winding staircase I walk onto an old tiled floor. Closed doors with writing on their opaque windows line both sides of the hall. Lucy and Annie didn't tell me where to find this guy, which office to go into. I don't even know which direction to go in as the staircase comes out in the middle of the hall. When one of the doors to my left opens, that makes my decision. I tiptoe in that direction hoping to find someone to talk to. First out the door is a large, gray trashcan on a wheeled cart, with mop handles sticking out the sides, and then the man who's propelling the cart comes through the door.

"Excuse me," I say, and the man's head lifts. I saw his muscular arms first, so I'm surprised to see he's an older gentleman.

"Hello, young lady. May I help you?" he asks in a low, mellow tone. His voice is the Old South incarnate, and I feel a swoon coming on.

"I hope so. I'm looking for Councilman Ray Barnette, and I forgot to find out which office is his."

"Would you by any chance have been sent on this errand by one lovely Lucy Fellows?" He steps from behind the cart and extends his hand. "And would that make you the most interesting newcomer carrying the distinguished name of Mantelle? Jewel Mantelle, I believe?"

I smile to keep from saying, in my best Scarlett O'Hara impression, "Charmed, I'm sure." I clear my throat but smile bigger as I lay my hand in his outstretched hand. "Yes. Yes, to everything."

He actually kisses my hand, then lays his other hand on top of it and winks at me. "Oh, darlin', don't go saying yes to everything a Southern man says. He might just forget his manners. Ray Barnette at your service."

I actually giggled as I pulled my hand back. But I did not flutter my eyelashes—at least I don't think I did.

He has a full head of white hair and is about my height, if not a few inches taller. He's wearing a maroon golf shirt and dark gray work pants. The logo on his shirt says "Plantation Services," and then I see the same logo on the side of the big trashcan. "Oh, Lucy said you worked here, and I, well, I assumed…"

"You assumed you'd find me behind one of these old doors of authority and many gilded words. I completely understand, but alas, no. This is my humble but necessary work. Now, how may I help you? Lucy said your husband is mixed up in the murder of Mr. Pierson Mantelle?"

He motions us over to a bench along the wall, and as I sit down, I shake my head. "Kind of. He, well, was on the docks yesterday, and the police did question him." I stall with my mouth ready to say something, but I can't think of what I need to know. Why did they send me of all people on this mission?

As he joins me on the bench, Mr. Barnette lets out a long low groan. "Yes, I, too, was questioned by our thorough Officer Greyson and the young Officer Bryant. Who would've imagined all this going so wrong? I'm only trying to help my beloved community, which does not have the resources to develop our marina as it could, and should, be developed. Pierson Mantelle agreed with me and I believe also had a true vision for the future of our beloved waterfront. Truly a magnificent vision, but will it ever happen now?" He shakes his head, lifts his hands in concern, and then lays one big hand on my shoulder. Maybe it's just a comforting pat, but I sit up straight anyway. When I look at him, he winks again and my cheeks flush.

As I shift away from his hand, I blurt, "So if his death stopped the idea of selling the marina, maybe that explains what happened. Who was most opposed to the idea?"

He shrugs and then waves his hands to indicate the offices around us. "Open any one of these doors and find at least one person who would lose some modicum of power and control if a private enterprise were to be engaged. Sophia may appear to be a small Southern island blessed with water, sand, and sun, but we are a town. A growing, thriving town, and there is lots of money to be made and power to be gained. I am only on the city council to provide a voice for common sense and reason." He stands up and pulls one of the mops from the bucket on the cart. "Yes, Mrs. Mantelle, I did meet with your husband's cousin, the newly departed Mr. Pierson Mantelle, yesterday on his boat. Did I kill him? No. He and I were allies in this struggle. Might I suggest you investigate the other council members to find the perpetrator of this vile crime? I had nothing whatsoever to gain in Pierson's death." One hand on the handle of the mop, he folds the other to his waist in a bow. "For now, dear lady, I must return to my duties before I lose this most needed job."

He unfolds from his bow and sweeps off down the dark hall.

I thank him and watch him enter another door. A janitor on the city council? That seems a little different, but why not? Why not, indeed. There's a large window at the end of the hall that lets in beams of morning light, and I think of all the drama this hallway has probably seen over the decades. It's so quiet and peaceful here, so I decide there's no hurry to report back to Annie. If she wanted to know what Mr. Barnette had to say, she should've come with me. She's the one that wants to play detective.

I settle back against the wooden slats of the old bench. It's surreal to find myself here. Not only on Sophia Island, but in this second-floor hallway of Sophia's historic courthouse. Especially given the circumstances that led me here. The murder of one of Craig's long-lost relatives? Bizarre. I let out a long breath, and my chest feels concave, empty. Finally I can think about what I've been trying not to think about. Why is my husband still lying to me?

Maybe even worse—why is he lying to the police? Can I put aside my guilt long enough to figure out his?

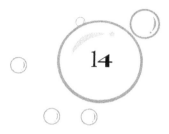

14

"I'm over here," Annie calls as I step over to the courthouse fountain, looking for her. "Over here in the shade."

She's sitting on a stone wall under some tall trees with smooth bark. They drape over her, and I have to stoop to join her on the seat. "What are these trees? The smooth trunks with the different coloring are really pretty."

She looks around her. "Oh, these are some really old crepe myrtles. See the ends of the branches there? Those are going to explode in flowers this summer. You don't have them up north?"

"I don't think so. Maybe I remember them from Tennessee, but the kids were little when we lived there so my recall about that time in my life isn't that great. Okay, so I met with your Mr. Barnette and—"

"Don't you be calling him *my* Mr. Barnette! What did Lucy tell you? She is such a blabbermouth. He didn't mention me, did he?"

Her eyebrows jump, lower, flatten, then jump again, and I can't help but laugh. "Oh, so you do like him? I thought he was very nice, very gentlemanly and gracious. Very Southern."

She narrows her eyes at me. "He's a big old flirt, and I'm too old for that nonsense. Besides, he might be a murderer!"

"But he explained that he and Pierson were on the same side," I say. "He thought we should look at the other councilmembers."

Annie lifts her purse onto her lap and rummages through it, pulling out her phone and the paper Eden gave her earlier. "That's what I thought also, so while you were inside playing footsies with that old degenerate, I was doing some real investigating." She looks up. "And don't roll your eyes at me, I've raised six teenagers. Eye rolling doesn't even faze me. Here's the list of the other councilmembers. Two are newcomers to town that I don't know, and I've not figured out a way to get information on them yet. There's Ray, and then there's the other two. One is Geo Clayton, who I know is out of town with his wife. Their grandchildren are on spring break up in North Carolina, so they took their RV up there for a couple weeks. The other is Sheryl-Lee King, and believe it or not, she was having lunch at Colby's yesterday, too. She's one of the people that came over to see Lucy as we were leaving."

Annie rubs her lips together as she looks around; then she leans toward me and whispers, "She was wearing a lime green suit, and the skirt was wet. You remember as we were walking out the door that Lucy stopped to talk to a woman?"

I match her whisper. "I do! She was coming out of the bathroom, and she said something about her skirt. It was really a bright green."

"Exactly! I remembered that as I was sitting here. Sheryl-Lee is plenty strong enough to hurl that pitcher at Pierson Mantelle. She's in her thirties and loves working out. Wonder if that stain on her skirt was margarita?"

"Oh, yes, it could be. Did you tell Aiden?"

She sits back and frowns at me. "Aiden? Let him get his own leads."

"Annie, no! This is not a mystery novel. Let the police do their job."

Her frown lightens, and she tilts her head. "And when are you going to tell the police that your husband is lying to them?"

I stand up, staying low to avoid the draping limbs. I stride past the fountain and onto the sidewalk before I stop and look back for Annie. Maybe I'm telling these ladies too much. Shouldn't I have Craig's back? But could there be more he's not telling me?

Annie's gathered everything and is carrying her purse, phone, and the paper from Eden jumbled in her arms. When she reaches me she holds out the paper. "Says right here your husband came to Colby's looking for you, but Lucy said you didn't know where we were having lunch until that morning. And you told us you hadn't talked to your husband in the past two days. That when he's on a jobsite he's hard to get hold of."

"I know. You're right. He is lying to the police, but here's the thing, Annie. He's also still lying to me. He told me just this morning he was there looking to have lunch with me. Does he not realize I know that he's lying? Does he think I'll lie to the police for him?" Tears fill my eyes, and a lump builds in my throat. "In his engineer mind, if you aren't thinking the way he's thinking, that's your problem. Or should I say *my* problem!" My throat shuts down with that lump, and the tears squeeze out as I clinch my eyes shut.

We stand on the sidewalk in silence for a moment, and then Annie reaches out to hug me. She's a good hugger, soft and intentional. Her hugs feel like she means them. As we separate my stomach growls. Loudly.

We laugh and she says, "I agree." With a wink directed at my stomach she says, "Speaking of lunch, do you want to meet another of my kids? Let's go this way."

"Alli-belle, you back here?" Annie says as we enter the nondescript concrete-block building from a back door. She whispers over her shoulder to me, "Alexandria is my free spirit. She's an artist this week."

"Momma? I'm in the front gallery."

We walk from the darkness toward the light coming in through high windows in the front. Little rooms along the hallway have walls covered in paintings. I remember coming into this gallery by way of the front entrance a week or so ago. There was a painting of a stork or a heron, one of those birds that stand in the water around here, which I really liked. I spot it in its same place on the side wall as a young woman walks over to us.

"I was just turning over the 'Closed for

Lunch' sign," she says in a grouchy voice, but her mother responds, all sunshine and sweetness.

"Perfect! I came to see if you wanted to go to lunch. This is my good friend Jewel, and I wanted her to meet you."

"Momma, cut out the charm. I know you think I can't afford to eat so you just happen to drop in at lunch or dinner to take me out. And since I don't have any food at home, yes, I'll go to lunch. We can go out the back door. I feel like Mexican."

We follow her back the way we came. She holds open the door for us, and as I pass by her she says, "Your name is Judy? Julie?"

"Jewel. With a W." I try to hold out my hand to her, but she pushes out and turns her back to us as she locks the door. She leads us off to the side, through some bushes on a little worn path. We come up on a gravel path that leads to the main street and a Mexican restaurant I hadn't been to yet.

She strides in the front doors, and we follow her through the restaurant toward the back. She slows down at the bar long enough to say a few words to the bartender, who obviously knows her; he nods and waves to me. Then he grabs Annie's arm and lifts her hand to kiss it. Annie introduces me, then laughs and points ahead of her, in the direction of her daughter who has left us behind. She and the bartender roll their eyes at each other. I think they share opinions on the latest Bryant child I've met.

I believe I could already share in that eye roll.

Alexandria has a table selected and is taking her seat in the huge outdoor patio behind the long, narrow restaurant. A big tree covers most of the area in shade, and I'm stunned that I never suspected this was back here. Before Annie and I are seated a waiter appears with our menus and glasses of water.

"Miss Annie and Miss Allie, good to see you both again."

Annie smiles up at the attractive young man and introduces me again.

He nods his head at me. "Miss Jewel. The Bryant ladies usually order our lunch combo of an enchilada, a taco, and shrimp salad. It is very reasonable and very good." He looks around the table. "Are we ready to order? No hurry."

Annie looks to her daughter. "Order whatever you'd like, Allie. Eduardo, I'm going to go with the lunch special."

The young woman picks up her menu and hands it to our waiter. "Eddie, give me two of the lunch specials. One to go. Guess that'll have to be dinner tonight."

"Lunch special for me also," I say.

"Any drinks to celebrate a new friendship?" he asks.

Annie and I shake our heads no, but Allie throws her hands up. "Sure. Bring me a margarita. It's not like there'll be any customers at the gallery the rest of the day. Who wants to spend a vacation day at the beach inside looking at cheap art?"

Eduardo nods, bows a bit, then turns, but as he does he says, "And I'll let Sheryl-Lee know you are out here, Miss Allie. I know she'd rather have lunch with you ladies than in her office."

Sheryl-Lee? The woman on the city council? The lady at Colby's yesterday?

Annie catches my eye and smiles. "Sheryl-Lee and Allie have been best friends for years. They went all through school together."

Allie sips her water as she slouches back in her chair. "Except I messed around taking college classes, and Sheryl-Lee got married before she turned nineteen. Thanks to her divorce she's now got a business and is on city council. Not exactly the horror story you thought it would turn into, was it, Momma?"

This time Annie's smile barely hides her gritting teeth, but there are no worries of her hurting Allie's feelings. Her daughter isn't giving her the time of day. Which might not be a bad thing.

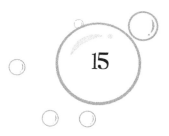

15

"Aren't they a matched set of gargoyle book-ends?" Annie says as she puts the last bite of taco in her mouth. We're finally alone at our lunch table.

Thank goodness.

I agree with my new friend. "They don't exactly make for good digestion. Sheryl-Lee sure has some strong opinions for such a young woman, doesn't she?"

Annie chews and nods as I lift a forkful of spicy shrimp salad to my mouth. As Eduardo had predicted, his boss joined us for lunch. Sheryl-Lee's lunch consisted of a basket of chips, extra-hot tomatillo sauce, and a huge margarita. Maybe the alcohol helped because she admitted to not only being on Pierson Mantelle's boat but to arguing with him because she thought his offer for privatizing the marina was way too low.

"He was just an old-fashioned shyster. The good old boy network in living color," she snarled. "I told him there were better offers out there for buying into the marina. He thought just because his name was Mantelle he had a foot—hell, a whole leg—already in the door. I shut that down!" By the time she'd finished her margarita and ordered another for her and Allie, Sheryl-lee was talking so fast and Annie and I were listening so hard that we barely remembered to eat, which is why we are still sitting here.

"This shrimp salad is so good. I really didn't know what to expect," I say.

"You can get it as an appetizer to eat with the chips, too," Annie says. "So, what did you think of Sheryl-Lee's explanation for what was on her skirt?"

"Didn't ring true, did it? She was talking, talking, talking, and then as soon as you mentioned that, she clammed up. She doesn't strike me as the kind of person that wouldn't know how her skirt got that wet."

Annie purses her mouth and nods. "I agree. When she said, 'Oh, someone spilt something on me,' she was definitely not telling the whole truth. You saw her. Can you imagine spilling something on her and her just brushing it off as no big deal?"

"More likely she'd flip the table and spear you with a fork. How in the world did she get elected to the city council?"

Annie shrugs. "Her daddy was on the council for years, right up until his death a couple years ago. I think when people saw the name King on the ballot, they assumed it was him. She took back her name after the divorce. At least she uses her bad attitude to get along in life. My Allie uses her bad attitude mainly to make people miserable. Here they come back," she says as she wipes her mouth with her napkin. The two younger women had excused themselves to the restroom and to chat with the bartender.

"I've got to get back to the gallery. Some old lady will call the owner if I'm not there to turn over the sign right at one o'clock," Allie says as she stands beside her friend. They look like spoiled, tipsy teenagers with their slouching, each one with a hand on her hip, the other hand messing with her hair. "Sheryl-Lee is coming with me to look at some pics for her new house. Can you believe she's buying a new house? On the beach?" She scowls at her mother. "Why did you make me go to college?"

Annie looks ready to explode, so I speak up. "There's a picture there I want to look at again, too. Do we pay our check on the way out?" I pull a twenty out of my billfold.

Sheryl-Lee picks up the checks and says, "Just give me the money and I'll take care of it."

Annie stands up and pushes my hand down. "Oh, I'm treating Jewel and paying with a card. Thanks for your help, Sheryl-Lee. We'll see y'all at the gallery in just a minute." She's all smiles again as she waves the young women to go on. Once they are back inside the restaurant she frowns. "Don't ever give that girl money. Skimming off the top comes as natural to her as swimming does to a fish."

"And she's on the city council?"

Annie takes one last sip of her water and says, "Yeah, but everyone knows, so they watch her." She squints those bright eyes at me. "Guess I should let Aiden know she was on Mantelle's boat?"

With a hard swallow, I croak, "Yes. Most definitely." I stand and follow her back into the restaurant and up to the bar where the man we saw earlier takes her card and my cash. I insisted on paying for mine. We're leaning on the bar waiting, and Annie's putting on lipstick. How do you get comfortable enough to put on lip-

stick without a mirror in a public place? It's
something I see women here doing all the time,
and I just don't know about it.

"Were you telling the truth about wanting to
look at a picture at the gallery?" she asks.

"Yes. I saw it a couple weeks ago. Why
wouldn't I be telling the truth?"

She shrugs and smiles. "Thought maybe you
were just being nice to Allie."

"No, not really. Does she get a commission
for what she sells?"

"No, but some sales might keep her sister
from firing her today."

"Her sister?" I ask as she puts her wallet back
together and we head toward the door.

"Amber. My daughter in real estate, where
we parked? She owns the gallery. The only way
Allie keeps gainfully employed is me begging my
other children to hire her. She's been at the gallery now almost three months. Might be some
kind of a record." She pushes the door open and
heads out into the sunshine.

Hmm, maybe it's not so bad not living near
my children.

At the gallery Annie and I examine the picture, and I decide I do want it. While I'm paying, she goes outside to call Aiden and catch him

up on all the leads she's following—her words, not mine.

Allie's too busy helping Sheryl-Lee to direct much negativity in my direction, so I linger and listen to the two friends discuss the pictures and the new house.

"Is it another part of the divorce settlement?" Allie asks. "Best thing you ever did, marrying Petey. Well, besides divorcing him."

"Catching him on the rebound from Sheila, he was ripe for the picking. But no, this money is from some work I've been doing. Nothing with the restaurant." She lowers her voice, but since I'm only across the small room from her I can hear her say, "I'm actually doing some work with Petey's father."

"No way! You had all the luck marrying into that family. Can you get me a job? I'm so sick of working for my brothers and sisters."

"Not that kind of work. But who knows? Might have a lot of job openings around here soon." As she comes around the corner of a rack of frames, Sheryl-Lee sees me. From the way her mouth clamps shut, I know she'd forgotten I was there.

Just at that moment, Annie sticks her head in the door. "Hey, you ready?"

"Sure. Bye, Allie and Sheryl-Lee. Nice to meet you," I say as I slip out the door.

Annie shakes her head at me a little and points down the sidewalk as I join her. Once we turn the corner headed to her car, she whispers, "Aiden didn't know Sheryl-Lee had even been on the boat! He said that boat had more traffic than the Atlanta airport on Thanksgiving weekend." She grasps my arm. "Oh, Jewel, we're really doing it! We're like real detectives." She's in a happy trance as we walk along to her car. "Wait till the girls hear this."

She's chattering along about all the clues as she drives me to my house. I'd planned on walking, but the picture is unwieldy to carry. As we come to my house, she pulls through the open gate and up to the front steps.

"Can't get used to them gates being open after being closed for so many years," Annie says. "We get this murder solved, and we can concentrate on helping you get your house in order. That's got to weigh on your mind something terrible, it being such a mess and all that junk. But that's what friends are for, right?"

The bright look on her face makes my chin start to quiver. "Really? You'll help me deal with all this?"

She leans toward me and pats my cheek.

"Well, of course, sweetie. You're one of us now."
A look of concern settles on her face. "Right?
Aren't you one of us? I mean, some people just
fit. You know?"

"I, uh, I guess. Sure." I open my door and
retrieve my painting from the back seat.

Before I can close the back door, she speaks
up. "Now you get in there and tell that husband
of yours that lying isn't the answer and you want
the truth. Then let me know what he says."

With a nod, I close the door. She waves and
pulls around the circle drive to leave the yard.

Tell Craig I want the truth.

Well, now, he's going to *know* that's a lie.

"Don't ask what you don't want to know"
was my mother's mantra. She'd gone to law
school when I, the younger of two, went into
first grade. My brother was three years older
than me. Mother took to heart the lawyer's di-
rective that you never ask a question of a witness
that you don't already know the answer to. She
would say it to me and my brother when we'd
ask pretty much anything. Even what was for
dinner. Often when we'd ask that question, she'd
repeat her mantra and then say, "Whatever you
decide to make for us. Call me when it's ready."

Sure, it made us rather self-sufficient, but it also made us leery of asking questions, which isn't always the healthiest life choice, especially when it comes to marriage.

Luckily Craig has always been a straight shooter. He says what he means and means what he says. Not a lot of questions were needed when we met, fell in love, and got married right after our college graduation. We had the twins only eleven months after we got married, and from that point on, I was just one tired, confused question. I relished a husband who would make all the big decisions. At first he seemed to want my opinion, but it didn't take long for him to realize I didn't have one. Asking just caused frustration on both our parts.

Plus, his onsite construction assignments meant he lived away from us most of the time. My military brother said he thought he was at home more than Craig, and he was probably right. I'm not sure why I thought us moving here would turn out well, but I sure didn't think we'd end up in this mess. A big sigh tries to work its way up and out, but I'm really getting tired of sighing, so I swallow it.

"Craig? Are you here?" I shout after I knock on his closed office door and get no answer. Walking around the downstairs, I listen but don't hear anything, which is nice. Sometimes the sounds in this house are downright creepy. I'm sure it's rodents in the attic, but there are times I could swear someone is upstairs. But old houses make noise, right?

With a shiver, I look out the back door to realize his car isn't in the driveway. I'm relieved he's not here. It's hard with him being gone so much, but after all, he never wanted to be here in the first place. Leaning against the door, I admit it: this whole mess is my fault. Why, when I finally stood up and had an opinion, did it have turn out so badly?

Pushing away from the door, I step purposefully toward the kitchen. I need to get my thoughts straight before I ask Craig about yesterday.

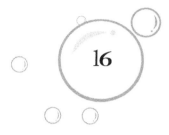

16

Pressing the flashing button on my coffeemaker means an immediate hit of sensory pleasure as a hot stream of chai tea fills my mug. The perfect afternoon pick-me-up. I lean over to smell it, then turn around to see if there's evidence of what Craig has been doing this morning. He's never been one to leave dishes out, so there's not much evidence of anything. He's so used to taking care of himself on the road that he does it at home as well.

When I got home from the gallery, I stood the picture of the tall bird in the water in a kitchen chair and leaned it against the wall so I could look at it. I study it now. It just looks so Florida. The sky behind the bird is pink and reflected in the water. It's not the ocean; there's no sand or waves. I guess it's the swamp? Or marsh?

Anyway, it wouldn't have fit in any other house I've lived in. Settled in across the table from it with my chai tea and a notebook, I start writing down what I know.

I first write the word "Suspects," but then I realize just how much that sounds like I am in an old-fashioned mystery show. I cross it out and write, "People who didn't like Pierson Mantelle." But then I think, did Craig like Pierson Mantelle? I don't know. Ray Barnette? Do you have to dislike someone to kill them, or just dislike what they might do? Or what they already did? Okay, fine. I tear off that sheet of paper and write "Suspects" at the top of the new sheet.

Ray Barnette. He said they were partners, but he was on the boat. What if Pierson Mantelle decided to pull out of buying the marina? What if Mr. Barnette tried to talk him into it and he'd gotten mad? What if Ray was going to make some money on the deal somehow? Being a janitor at his age may mean he needs money. He did mention something about needing that job, and with those arms, he could definitely wield that margarita pitcher.

Sheryl-Lee. She definitely did not like Pierson Mantelle, and I have no trouble seeing her swinging the pitcher at him, or anyone, if she was mad. But she was so open about her hostility towards him. Wonder if she'll be so open with the police? She did say she had "put a stop to that." So just how did she put a stop to Mr. Mantelle's plan for the marina? She also mentioned to Allie more jobs or something like that. Did she have her own plan for the waterfront?

Girlfriend of Mr. Mantelle. I know the police say she and her friend were too drunk, but having raised two girls and experienced dozens of their friends, I know that girls that age can be pretty good at lying and acting helpless when they need to. They can also be freakishly strong when they want to be. I mean, have you ever tried to take a phone out of a teenage girl's hand?

Aiden told his mother there'd been a lot of people on the boat. Wonder who else?

Craig? He said he wasn't, but then he lied about looking for me at the marina.

From my seat at the table I can see at an angle out the back door to Craig's office door. Maybe I should go look inside. I don't know if it's hanging out with the lunch bunch and their detective talk, or maybe it's knowing for the first time in our marriage that Craig is lying to me. Maybe I'm crazy, but I have an overwhelming feeling I need to go in there.

I move before I can change my mind. At the door out of the kitchen I stop and look both ways. Yuck, that feels too sneaky. This is my house. I'm across the hallway, and my hand is turning the doorknob before I can let my mind think of anything else.

The room is warm. And it's a mess. Papers are laying all over Craig's desk and on the floor. His briefcase is open and half falling off a stack of boxes. Out of the corner of my eye a sudden movement makes my heart stop. I jerk back behind the door, but then my mind registers what the movement was. The curtain is moving. Ducking around the door, I see that the back window is wide open. That's why the room is warm. When I venture back in I'm shaking my head because this can't be what it looks like. I mean, it looks like a break-in. Like someone came in that window and made this mess because they were looking for something. That's why all the drawers in the desk are wide open, one even upside down on the floor.

That's when it hits me. Oh my goodness. We've had a break-in! I step back, slam the office door, and run across the kitchen to the table where my purse is. I pull out my phone and dial 911. Then I have to sit down because my knees have suddenly turned to jelly. A much-used phrase, though one I've just discovered is completely accurate.

"Hello, this is Jewel Mantelle, and we've been broken into." I rush to confirm the operator's question. "Yes, the Mantelle house." Then my blood turns to ice—another descriptive phrase I didn't realize was true. "Still in the house? I don't know. I, uh. Yes, *I'm* in the house."

The 911 dispatcher tells me to leave the house, and now my jelly knees are like concrete. I force myself to stand. The front door seems so far away, but the open window was to the back of the house. Wouldn't it be better to not go out that way? The woman is talking, but I'm trying to decide where to escape to. Just as I start toward the front door, it opens and my knees are back to jelly. Luckily I'm beside the counter, so I lean on it as I yell into the phone, "Someone's coming in the door!"

"Jewel? Are you okay?" Craig calls. I turn to see him running toward me. "What's going on? Who are you talking to?"

I grab him and push him back the way he came. "We've got to go outside. Hurry!" On the porch I slam the door behind us and jog down the front steps to collapse onto the foot-high wall along the drive. Here I can breathe.

Craig sits beside me on the old cement wall. "What is going on? Are you okay?"

"We've had a break-in," I gasp. "Your office.

Back window is open and it's a mess. Papers everywhere."

He stands up, but I grab his hand. "No! The 911 lady said they could still be in there. Look, there's the police!"

Two men jump out of their car with guns drawn. I then realize the 911 operator is trying to get my attention on my phone. I lift it to hear her exclaim, "She's in the house with the intruder!" Then she shouts, "Mrs. Mantelle, are you okay?"

"Oh, yes. I'm okay. It was my husband coming in the front door." I shout to the officers, "This is my husband. He's not the intruder." Back into the phone I say, "The officers are here. Thank you so much. I've never had to call 911 before."

The operator assures me that the officers on the scene will handle everything and that she's glad she could help. Craig is on the lawn talking to the officers when another police car pulls up and Aiden and Officer Greyson jump out. The first two policemen move on to check out the house. Aiden and Craig stop when they get to me.

"Let's move out toward the street to talk," Aiden says.

I stand and lean on Craig while my knees try

to return to normal. "Now that I think about it, I was in the house for quite a while before I realized there'd been a break-in, so I don't think there's anyone in there. But your office is a mess."

Aiden pulls out a pad, then looks up and says, "Oh no," as his mother's car screeches to a stop on the road outside. The first police car had pulled into our drive and is parked in the way of the entrance.

Annie flings her door open and jumps out, but when she sees me, she clutches her chest and bends over for a moment. "Thank the Lord!" she shouts as she starts towards us. "When I heard there was a break-in on the scanner, I about broke my neck getting here. Are you okay?" She's wearing a crisp, lime-green shirt over her bathing suit. Her bathing suit is black with white and lime-green trim. She has on cute flip-flops with big green flowers on them and a white floppy hat with a black, lime, and white scarf tied around it that trails behind her as she hurries. She looks like she's just stepped out of a magazine, one of those plus-size models, and just seeing her makes my heart start calming down.

Aiden meets her halfway to us, but she ignores him. "Me hugging my friend won't impede your investigation one bit. Honey, I bet you were scared to death!"

I get one of Annie's deep hugs, and then she doesn't miss a beat when she turns to Craig and pulls him to her. Aiden and I share a look, then a grin at Craig's surprise. She steps back and apologizes. "I don't normally run around on the city streets in my swimwear, but I was just headed over to Adam's house to play in the sprinklers with his kids when I heard. Lord help us, what if I'd already been gone?" She turns to Aiden. "How do I get a scanner for my car? Can I get one of them things y'all carry around with you?"

"Mrs. Bryant," Officer Greyson says as he walks up on us. "Hate to see we interrupted your swimming, but we have everything handled here. We just need to talk to the Mantelles, so you can return to whatever you were doing."

"I do need to get to my son's home as I'm watching the children this afternoon, but don't you worry, Jewel, Cherry will be right over. She was off the island shopping, but she's headed here right this minute. I mean, we all know this has something to do with Pierson Mantelle's murder, don't we?"

My mouth drops open, and as I look around I realize I'm the only one who didn't know that. Craig's mouth is in a tight line, Aiden is doodling on his pad, and Officer Greyson grunts. No one is meeting my eyes.

"Is she right?" I ask. "Is this connected to the murder? Why?"

Annie steps back into the middle of the group and hugs me. "That's exactly what we're going to find out, darling. See, there's Cherry now." She steps toward Craig, but he steps back and sticks a hand out. Whether it's to block her or shake her hand I can't tell, but Annie grabs it with both her hands and squeezes. "Now you take care of your wife. I'll let Abigale know what's going on over here in case you need your lawyer for anything, okay?"

Craig tries to step back as he shakes his head. "No, no need to call your daughter. I let her know she doesn't need to worry about us."

Annie is still clutching his hand; she looks at me and raises an eyebrow. "I'm assuming you two didn't get a chance to talk yet?"

My eyes widen, and I shake my head quickly.

Aiden says, "Mother," and Officer Greyson says, "Annie," at the same time with the exact same inflection.

"All right, all right." She releases Craig's hand and steps away. She says a few words to Cherry, and the officers take that moment to shepherd us back toward the front steps.

One of the first two officers has walked out onto the porch and waved that all is clear inside.

"We can go inside to talk, okay?" the older officer said. "Mr. Mantelle, we need you to take a look in your office and see if you can tell if anything is missing."

As we head inside, I ask Craig, "Where were you? I thought you were working here today."

He whispers, "Later," and steps ahead of me to run up the porch steps. Behind him I see the officers meet eyes. Aiden's eyebrows rise, and Officer Greyson grunts again.

Just as Cherry lays her arm across my shoulder, it hits me.

My husband is still a murder suspect.

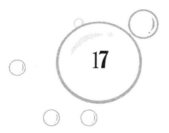

17

Cherry and I are about the same height, so her arm is able to stay on my shoulders as we walk up the front steps. The front door is not quite closed, so we push it open and step inside. As I begin to close it one of the police officers says, "Ma'am, I wouldn't close that if I were you. Nigh impossible to open. Hmm, maybe we should fingerprint it? Maybe it was damaged by the burglar."

As I pull it to, I tell him, "It's been that way since we moved in. Do you think the burglar was here or in the rest of the house?"

Officer Greyson steps out of the office and walks toward us. "No, we don't, but we'll keep looking. Maybe you can look around and see if you notice anything out of place? But first, tell me what time you left this morning and when you arrived home."

"Okay. Can I get some water?" I walk into the kitchen. As I enter, I see the list I'd been working on, with the "Suspects" written in big, bold, embarrassing letters at the top. I dart to the table and pick up the pad, folding it shut, then hold it close to me as I go to the fridge. "Can I get anyone else a bottle of water?"

Cherry shakes her head; so does the officer. Then he says, "We can just sit here if that's okay."

As I slide into a chair, I push the notebook onto the empty chair seat beside me. "Okay. I left here this morning sometime before ten. Annie may know exactly what time. She came over to get me, and we went the coffee shop to meet Lucy Fellows. After that we shopped some, then talked to some people, had lunch with Annie's daughter Allie, then I bought that painting." I point at it. "Then I came home. I don't remember what time it was exactly. Again, Annie may have noticed. Oh, Allie had to get back to the gallery by one, so it wouldn't have been too long after that."

"Once you got home, what did you do?" the officer asks. "Did you go upstairs or out back? I'm assuming you came in the front as you would've noticed the open window if you'd used the back door."

"Yes, if I don't park around back, I use the front door. Now that I've learned how to open it, it's not a problem. No, I didn't go upstairs to change. That's why I'm still in this dress."

Cherry laughs. "Whew, that's a relief. I was thinking, 'If that's what she wears to hang around the house, we can't be friends.'"

That one comment and her laugh release a knot of tension along my shoulders, and I smile at her. Looking back to Officer Greyson, I point at the cold cup of tea sitting in front of him. "I made that cup of tea, then sat down here… thinking. Then, for some reason, I got up and went to look in Craig's office." I look down and feel the tension working its way back along my neck.

"And what did you find there?"

"It was warm, and there were papers every-where. The curtains moving scared me, and that's when I realized the window was open. I ran back here to get my phone out of my purse, and I called 911. First time ever." I take a drink of my water. "She, the 911 lady, told me to get out of the house, so I was trying to decide which way to leave when Craig came in the front door. Scared me to death! Scared the 911 operator, too, when I screamed someone was coming in to the house." I grimace, thinking of her panicked voice. "Poor woman. The first police car showed up really fast, and then you and Officer Bryant got here. That's it."

"Was your husband still here when you left this morning?"

"Yes, he was working from home today because, well, I guess you told him to stay close?"

The officer ignores my question. "So you didn't hear anything when you got home?"

"No. I don't know how long Craig had been gone. I suppose he went to get some lunch. We haven't had a chance to chat. I bet he's upset about his office. I should check on him." I stand up and Cherry does, too, but Officer Greyson motions for us to sit back down. As we do Cherry reaches out and takes my hand in hers.

The officer explains, "They'll be done in there in just a minute. So you were sitting here thinking before you opened the office door?" His eyes shift to the chair next to me, where I'd slid the notebook. "Just thinking? Not writing anything?"

Of course he saw my notes when he was in here earlier. I'm not a good liar, and Cherry just stays quiet. Where's Annie and all her bluster when you need it? "I might've been writing down some stuff. Nothing important."

He tips his head and looks at me from under his bushy eyebrows. "Mrs. Mantelle, help me out here. We're not used to murders on Sophia, and we'd like to get this one solved as soon as possible. Isn't that what you want, too?"

When I pull out the notebook, Cherry releases my hand so I can open it. I flip to the page with "Suspects" written in big letters. My friend lets out a little gasp as she sees what's written below the heading.

The officer takes the offered notebook and reads it. "Y'all've been busy, haven't you? This Sheryl-Lee is Sheryl-Lee King, the one on the city council, I assume? Do you know something I don't about her?"

"Well, Annie told Aiden earlier, right?" He barely nods. "Sheryl-Lee was on Mr. Mantelle's boat yesterday. She really didn't like him, I guess. Stuff about the marina. And her skirt was wet when we saw her at Colby's after lunch."

He makes some notes in his own notebook, then scowls again at my sheet. "Ray Barnette? And did you run into him while you were shopping?"

Okay, there's that tension in my neck that

was trying to get away. "Not exactly. I ran into him in the courthouse."

He squints at me. "Your notes say that 'he said he needed this job'?" He looks at me. "Said he 'needed' it?"

"Yes, I mean, that's understandable. Janitors don't make that much."

Cherry pats my hand and clears her throat. "We'll talk about Mr. Barnette in a minute."

"Just another question or two, Mrs. Mantelle. Here beside your husband's name you've written 'LIE.' In caps. What does that mean? What did he lie about?"

Cherry leans forward, breaking Officer Greyson's direct line of sight to me. She looks me in the eyes. "Honey, you don't have to answer that. These are just your personal doodles. They don't have to mean a thing."

Taking a deep breath, I nod. "She's right. It didn't mean anything. Just, just doodling."

He lumbers to his feet and lays my notebook back down on the table. "Whatever you say, Mrs. Mantelle. However, I think you should know I'm pretty sure the burglar was in the office when you came home. Looks like they were in a big hurry to leave and fell out the back window instead of stepping over to the back porch as they apparently did coming in."

I shudder. Cherry's smile at me is weak. My knees don't return to their jelly state, but the officer's words definitely make them quiver. There are voices outside the office door, and soon Officer Greyson is standing in the kitchen, holding out his hand to me. "Thank you, Mrs. Mantelle. Remind your husband to fix that back window."

Shaking his hand I ask, "Did they break it getting in?"

"No. It doesn't lock. Slides right up and needs a stick in it to prop it open. You probably didn't have time to notice that there was a stick in it when you went in there."

"So they broke the lock?" My hand is still in his, but the way he's looking at me has me almost transfixed. It's like he's trying to tell me something.

"No. The lock didn't work before. It hasn't worked in a long time."

"Oh wow. We had no idea."

He squeezes my hand once more and lets it drop. "Your husband knew." He stares at me for just another fraction of a second and then turns to shake Cherry's hand. "Good to see you again, Mrs. Berry."

"Wait," I say. "Your name is Cherry Berry?"

She grimaces. "Yep. Until we had kids I kept my maiden name, but then I decided, 'Who wouldn't want to be one of the Berrys when those babies are so cute?'" She shakes the grinning officer's hand. "At least no one ever forgets my name."

Distant voices grow louder as the men come into the kitchen. Cherry puts her arm back around my shoulders. As the officer working with Craig lays out some papers on the counter, I pull Cherry toward the living room. Once we're out of the kitchen door, though, I lead her to the right, and we walk quietly down the hall to the office.

We tiptoe in and look around. The window is closed again. I look out of it. The porch, more of what we called a stoop up north, is just to the side of the window. I think I could even lean over the wooden railing, open the window, and climb onto it. I'd never thought about it, but if I'd known this window didn't lock, I think I would've. I can't decide if I'm more scared or mad. I've been here alone several nights, and Craig knew it wouldn't lock?

Cherry whispers, "Is anything is missing?"

"I don't know. I've only been in here a half dozen times. Craig's the only one who would know."

Aiden sticks his head in the room. "Mrs. Mantelle? We're leaving now. I just wanted to say goodbye and that I'm real sorry this happened. You get that window fixed, you hear? We stuck a piece of wood in the top to hold it shut for now. My momma will be worried about you. Matter of fact, she's probably half melted my personal phone by now, but I left it in the car." He winks at me. "No need for you to tell her, though, okay?"

"Okay. Thank you so much and tell Annie not to worry. I'm sure we'll be fine now." He pulls away from the door, but I stop him. "Aiden? Could this have just been some kids? Someone looking for some money or something? It doesn't have to be related to the murder, does it?"

He steps in closer and shakes his head as he thinks. "In some ways that would be comforting, I know. But it just seems awful coincidental, doesn't it? A Mantelle is murdered one day and a Mantelle is burgled the next? My momma says, 'You ignore what's right in front of your face and you deserve what you get.' Momma may be a pain, but she sure ain't stupid." He tips his head to me as he leaves the room.

Cherry is squatting down looking at cords plugged into a power strip on the floor beside the desk.

"What are you looking at?" I ask her.

"Nothing." She straightens up. "Anything else you want to look at in here?"

"No. I want to get out of this dress, take a long shower, and have a glass of wine."

She gives me a one-armed side hug as she scoots out of the door before me.

I look around at Craig's office and quietly add an item, the most important item, to my to-do list. "And then I want to talk to my husband."

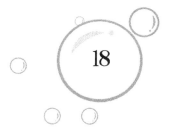

18

By the time the police all leave, shadows are lengthening in the front yard and throughout the house. "I'm starving," I say to Craig as we stand in the living room, still kind of stunned. "I had plans for hamburgers on the grill, but that sounds like too much work now. How about soup and a sandwich? Of course, I have a frozen pizza for such a crazy day as this. Want that?"

He leans to give me a kiss on my cheek. "It has been a strange one, hasn't it?"

Before I can lean into him, he pulls back and walks away. "However, I do have to return some calls for work. This afternoon was shot. Put the pizza in, and if I'm not done by the time it's ready, I can eat it later. Thanks." He's in his office and closing the door before I can get fully turned around or think of what to say.

Watching him, the churn of hunger in my stomach turns into a churn of anxiety. When I walk into the kitchen, my eyes fall on my new painting. I stop to look at it. The pinks of the sky and the steadiness of the bird calm me, and I take a deep breath. "A really hot shower. That's what I need," I say as I walk farther into the kitchen to preheat the oven. At the fridge, I grab an already opened bottle of pinot grigio and pour myself a glass for the shower.

Craig's voice rises and falls from his office, and it's hard to imagine everything that happened here today. As I walk up the stairs the window on the landing that faces west, toward the river beyond the marina, is lit up with a shaft of light from the lowering sun. I stop to sip my wine and watch the sun shoot through the leaves and Spanish moss that wrap around our house. We need to make more of an effort to get down to the marina to watch the sunset. As I turn to finish walking up the stairs, I sigh. I'm sure Pierson Mantelle never thought Tuesday's sunset was his last.

My shower made all the difference. I dashed down the stairs earlier and put the pizza in the oven while I was only wrapped in a towel, then hurried back up to the bedroom. Now I'm ready to get everything straightened out with Craig. And eat. It seemed too early to put on my pajamas, so I threw on a pair of shorts and an old baseball shirt from my son Drew's high school team. I listen for Craig's voice while I throw together a salad, but I don't hear him. That's a good sign. He's getting his work wrapped up. Him working on the road all these years was hard, but it was almost harder to have him home because he would always bring work home at the end of the day. I'd expect him to be with us, but instead he'd be holed up in his home office. I'd make nice family meals, and he'd eat them later. Without the family. Basically, it was a lot less frustrating for him to just be on the road.

Last year, when our youngest, Drew, went off to college, was eye-opening for me. At the same time Erin—the older twin and the child I talk to most often—moved away to St. Louis with her husband. We'd lived in Geneva, a beautiful town outside Chicago, for only three years. Our first year had been filled with Erin's wedding and Chris's senior year in his and Drew's new school. Both girls were out of college and on their own by the time we moved to Geneva, although they both still lived in the Chicago area. We celebrated Chris's graduation and his move to college as we ended our first year there. After he left, with Drew's baseball schedule and his high school activities and friends, my life was still busy. I loved having a houseful of his friends at any time. Craig's life through all these changes moved on as usual, except the higher up he moved, the more challenging and time-consuming his projects became.

The house got really quiet really quick when Drew followed his brother to the University of Wisconsin in May, when he left early for the summer semester. I floundered around, not sure what to do with myself. Then in the fall Craig's latest project ended in a bit of mess, so he was at loose ends at work. This house falling into our laps after the new year sounded like just the new start Craig and I needed.

"Craig? The pizza is in, and I made a salad," I say, following up with a little knock on his office door. It's funny how this brings back this afternoon. I hesitate at turning the doorknob. "Craig?"

When I open the door, the office is empty. Not ransacked this time, but still empty. I leave the door standing wide open and step to the back door. I open it and look out to see that his car is gone once again.

"This is absurd!" I slam the back door. At the

kitchen counter I stand with both hands planted in front of me, trying to calm down. I don't know when I've been this mad. Our counselor kept saying that was an issue—that I never got mad.

Just as the timer on the oven starts beeping, my phone rings. I turn off the oven timer and step to my phone. It's Annie. Another thing our counselor said often was that I needed to make some friends. That I needed to get my own life.

I pick up the phone, hit the green answer button, and start talking. "Annie, want to come over for some pizza and wine? I have to warn you it's frozen pizza and, well…" As my steam runs out I realize of course she has something better to do. She has all those adorable grandchildren, friends, and church activities.

"Hallelujah!" she says. "I was looking for some excuse to not play another round of Candyland. I'll be right there. Wait, should I call the other girls? Have a real detectives' meeting? Oh, I think we should."

I'm grinning so widely that I don't realize at first that I'm just nodding, not answering. "Yes! Yes, that would be great. Oh, I have salad, too!"

"Perfect. I'll be there quick as a bunny!"

The phone is still in my hand when I wonder what will happen if Craig comes home. What if he wants to talk—just the two of us? What if he's tired and doesn't feel like company? Then the 'what ifs' are cut off with a look at my bird painting.

"No," I say firmly. "Stop thinking like that. Craig left no note, didn't text me, didn't wait for me. He left with a pizza in the oven. He couldn't even walk up the stairs to tell me where he was going." I put another bottle of wine in the refrigerator after refilling my glass with the opened one.

I turn off the oven and set up plates, bowls, and utensils on the counter. This all feels so familiar, but how can it? I never entertained. Then I realize I entertained the kids' friends all the time. I loved having a house full of teenagers, loved cooking for them and serving them. When I hear banging on the front door, I pick up my glass and head in that direction, where a new friend waits on the other side. With a tip of my glass I say to the air, and to our counselor, "Here's to you, Dr. Kahill. You'd be so proud."

Tamela pulls a bottle of wine from her big bag. "Grabbed this when I got Annie's group text. If we don't drink it this time, then we'll have it for next time." She sets it on the counter.

It's a big bottle, so it's heavy for her to haul up and onto the counter. She really is tiny.

Annie helps her. "Give me that before you hurt yourself! Lucy is having Davis drop her off here on their way home. They always go out to Shelley's on Thursdays for cheap oyster night."

Cherry already has a plate of pizza and salad. "Where do you want us to eat?"

"Wherever is good with me. Living room? I can't say we don't have enough tables and chairs. Sit anywhere. So Davis, that's Lucy's boyfriend, right?"

"Yes," Tamela says as she heads to the living room. "He's richer than God and better-lookin', if my Sunday School upbringing is correct. You can bet I wouldn't be leaving him to come hang out with us. Especially if he's just had a meal of raw oysters!"

Annie follows her friends into the living room. "Tamela, you left Hert home alone to be here."

Tamela rolls her eyes from her seat on the ornate velvet chair in the corner. Her feet are set on a matching velvet stool, and she looks like a posed doll. "We finished dinner early, and Hert is downstairs working on some new carpentry project."

"Your husband's name is Hurt?" I settle into

my usual spot on the couch. Everyone has made themselves at home and found tables to set their things on. Granted they've had to push aside stiff, plastic doilies and an assortment of ceramic animals, mostly birds, to make room.

"Not with a U but with an E, since it's short for Hubert. He's been Hert as long as I've known him."

Cherry is sitting next to me, digging into her food. "This is delicious, Jewel. My husband is always trying to lose weight and so I try to help by cooking healthy, but I feel like I'm starving half the time."

Annie stops before she takes a bite of the piece of pizza she's holding up. "I hate people like you. You probably lose more on his diets that he does. That's how my husband was. Bill could eat all day and night and never gain an ounce. Of course, he did run around like you do, Cherry. Couldn't sit still a minute."

Cherry clears her throat, chews a couple times, then looks around the room. "Speaking of husbands," she asks me, "where's yours?"

I pause from taking a bite of pizza. "I don't know. He was making some work calls when I went up to take a shower, and by the time the pizza was ready he had left. His car is gone, and he's not answered my text."

"He hasn't answered your text?" Tamela says, concern filling her voice. "I hope he's okay."

Grease from the pizza makes it easy to slide my lips back and forth without opening my mouth. I've never realized how not having friends makes it much easier to not acknowledge the sticky spots in life. They are all looking at me, so I say it. "He never—well, not never—but rarely answers my texts. It's pretty much always a one-way conversation."

And there it is. I'm seeing Craig through other people's eyes. I set my plate on the coffee table. Suddenly I'm full. Trying to fix it a bit, I add, "But I'm used to that."

Cherry says, "Okay. Good to know. We won't worry about him. That makes it easier to talk, really. Him not being here." She keeps eating, but I can see she's thinking. We all wait to hear what she's coming up with. "Couple things. Tamela, you're not eating, can you take some notes?"

"Sure!" Tamela has a purse strapped around her. From it she pulls a small notepad and pen. "One thing I miss about teaching is writing stuff down. I have drawers full of these little notepads."

Our attention is pulled to the front door. We hear footsteps coming up the steps and across the porch. "It's me," Lucy says as she attempts to open the door.

I'm already up and headed that way. "Good to see you, Lucy. There's pizza and salad, but I guess you've just come from dinner? There's also wine."

"Wine will be divine. You sit back down and eat. I can take care of myself." She flies by me in a hot-pink sundress. Her blonde hair is fluffed up higher than usual, and she smells like a piña colada. I follow her but see she's already found a glass and is opening the refrigerator by the time I get there.

She shoos me away. "Go eat. I'll be right there. You are such a doll having us over here like this. All I can think about is this case. You know the longer we go without solving this, the less likely it is that it will ever be solved."

She's shortly behind me as we go back into the living room. She sits in one of the straight chairs near the hallway, and as she crosses her legs, Annie moans.

"Look at those adorable shoes! How do you prance around here wearing those?"

Lucy sticks out a leg. "Aren't they pretty? It just takes practice. I feel like I trip over my own two feet when I wear flats." She angles her foot so the light shines off the white heels with silver and white straps, then drops her pretty foot with its pink toenails to swing as she says, "So. What did I miss?"

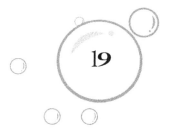

19

Lucy's foot stops bouncing as she blurts, "Oh, the break-in! Annie's text said someone broke into your house, Jewel? How? Where? What did they take? You weren't here, were you?"

Swallowing the bite of salad I'd forced on my queasy stomach just isn't happening easily, so I motion for Cherry to tell her.

"No one was here. They really didn't have to break in; the window in her husband's office doesn't actually lock and is within reach of the back porch." Cherry looks at me. "Did your husband say anything about that? Why he left it like that?"

"He knew?" Tamela yelps. "Lord, I love our security system. I'm a big ol' scaredy-cat. I'd kill Hert Stout if he left me alone with an unlock-able window."

Wow, this is harder than I thought, this seeing Craig through others' eyes. I shove the last bit of limp lettuce aside and admit, "Well, we actually didn't get to talk about it. He had some work to do, and then he was gone."

Lucy tilts her head and frowns. "Gone where?"

"I don't know." Excuses come to mind, but I leave them there. The women all look away from me for a moment, pretending to be engaged in eating or drinking.

Cherry sits her glass on the table in front of us and turns toward me. "Jewel, does Craig have two laptops?"

"Um, maybe? I assume he has one for work, and I know he bought one last year. I just use my tablet, so I don't know if he uses them both or if he still has a work one since we moved. Why?"

"I'm asking because the cords on his desk looked like they were for two different laptops. I know because I'm constantly changing out cords for laptops now that our daughter is living with us. She has absolutely no respect for my things being plugged in." She rolls her eyes and waves a hand. "But don't get me started on that. Anyway, last thing I heard from the police when they were leaving is that nothing is missing, and yet there was only one laptop I could see."

"But surely if the thief took Craig's laptop, he'd have noticed." I look around the room for support, but I'm met with only skeptical stares. "Wouldn't he?"

"Good place to start thinking," Lucy says. "If he does have a second laptop and it was stolen, why wouldn't he want the police to know?"

"Something on it he doesn't want them to see?" Tamela asks. "Or maybe he knows who took it?"

Annie shrugs. "Or maybe he just leaves it in the car like my kids do with their phones when they don't want to answer my calls."

I can't help but grin. "Aiden doesn't think you know he does that."

Annie winks. "Never let on what all you know to your kids. It's so much easier if they think you are a bit stupid. So, it could be as simple as that. Just left it in the car."

"No," I say with a sigh. "Craig is way too security conscious for that. He never leaves anything important in the car. I've even known him to go back out to his locked car at night because he left a jacket in it. He was raised in a not-so-good neighborhood. He would never leave a laptop in his car."

"Wait," Cherry interjects. "Maybe it was in the car because *he* was in the car. He wasn't here when the break-in happened. Where was he?"

I shrug. "Again, I don't know." This time they don't look away. "But that's right. It could've been with him. If he even has a second computer."

Lucy puts both feet on the floor and leans forward with both hands wrapped around her glass. "What I want to know is how would the sale of the marina have anything to do with a break-in here? I've been looking into all of that today, and it looks mighty fishy, no pun intended. The projections on anticipated earnings are over the moon—at least the ones Pierson Mantelle had put together for his company were. It's a booming reality all over the state that public marinas can't afford to keep up with regulations, especially if they need to do repairs or expand. So a private company comes in, fixes everything up, and charges ship owners accordingly."

"Some of the regulations are from a long time ago and need to be loosened," Tamela says, "but no one will touch anything, right? At least that's what my neighbor Anton Murkowsky said."

"Hey," Annie says as she sits up straight. "He's a councilmember. One of the newcomers I didn't know how to get hold of."

Tamela laughs. "Annie, he's lived here almost ten years."

"Like I said, a newcomer. What's he like? Is he married? I don't think I know his wife—I'd remember that name."

We all laugh. It's nice to laugh; it's also nice for them to not be looking at me.

Tamela shakes her head. "He's not married, but he has a girlfriend from down south somewhere. He's retired, early I think, but she's not, so she is only here on the weekends." She smiles innocently. "I just *happened* to walk my dogs same time as him this morning. He said he got involved in city matters because he saw what happened in South Florida, with the rapid building everywhere. He was pretty worked up about how few public marinas are left down there now."

Lucy nods. "Yes, he's got quite a following in town. Well-spoken, knowledgeable, well-versed on the environmental side, which adds some balance to the board. He has a tendency toward hair-on-fire excitement, but it does burn itself out rather quickly with him. Pun intended," she says with a wink. "But I don't think he'd be the type to hit someone over the head and kill them."

"I agree," Tamela says as she stands up to

stretch. "However, he said he *was* downtown yesterday. His dogs looked newly groomed. He said he'd dropped them off at the Animal House yesterday morning and picked them up after lunch. He had lunch at the Turtle Shell, not as close to the marina as Colby's, but right there. Ladies, I'm going to have to go. Early morning tomorrow." She groans as she plants her hands on her hips. "Hert and I are trying yoga."

Annie laughs. "Hert doing yoga? Let me guess, you mentioned you were going to try it, and next thing you know, he's doing it, too?"

"Yes. I know I shouldn't complain, but he has no idea what to do with himself. He had no intention of retiring so soon, and his woodworking projects are not as much fun as he thought, and I hoped, they'd be."

Cherry also stands up and picks up her plate. She's muscled and moves with a powerful grace. I've always envied the way athletes move, though not enough to actually be athletic. "You'll love yoga," she says. "Just stick with it, and it'll be good for both of you. Lucy, do you need a ride home?"

"Yes. I told Davis one of you would bring me home," she says as she finishes the last sip of her wine.

"Home?" Annie asks. "Home as in your home? Where Davis is now?"

"Good try, Annie, but no, Davis and I are not living together. He's at the Isle, and I'm going home to mine and mother's."

I follow the three into the kitchen, leaving only Annie still seated in the living room. "Your mother lives here?"

Lucy smiles. "Yep, she's a sweetheart. You'll have to come over for lunch one day and meet her. She doesn't get out much, but she loves our house on the beach, so she's happy."

"Oh, you live on the beach! How nice."

"My parents bought the house forty years ago and rented out the upstairs apartment. That's where I live now." She bends to the side to look back in at Annie as she says loudly, "All. By. Myself." She turns to me with a shake of her head. "Annie's obsessed with Davis's and my relationship because her beau is tired of dating and wants to marry her."

A chorus of oohs is accompanied by all of us coming back toward the living room.

"Wait, is it Ray Barnette? The man I talked to today? The jan—" I pause at his occupation, but Annie finishes it.

"Yes, the janitor and now murder suspect. That is the only way I want to discuss him." She pushes up out of the deep chair she'd chosen. "This detective stuff is hard. So what did we figure out tonight?"

We all stand in place and think, but no one seems to come up with anything.

Lucy finally admits, "Maybe I've had too much wine, but I know we must've come up with something. It feels late, doesn't it?"

"I know," Tamela says tapping her notebook. "I'll type up everything I wrote down and send it to you all tonight. Lucy, you have Jewel's email, so you can just forward it to her. Let's all look it over and then talk again."

Cherry ruffles her short hair. "My shift at the hospital starts at seven tomorrow night, but I'm free until then. With Martin working from home now, it's good for me to be out of the house during the day."

"Good thought," I say. "I've never had Craig working from home during the day. It *is* kind of weird."

"I know!" Lucy chirps. "Y'all come to Mother's for lunch. I'll pick up salads from Island Deli, which is what I usually do on Friday anyway since I'm at the senior center until noon." She pulls herself up straight, and although she's wearing a hot-pink sundress and strappy stilettos, she looks in charge. "Jewel, find out everything you can from your husband. Especially about the possibility of his owning another laptop. Annie, get more from Aiden. And why don't you break down and call Ray to see what he'll tell you about any possible marina deal. Tamela, talk to your neighbor to tighten up whether he actually has an alibi. I think we also have to look more into those bimbos on the boat with Mr. Mantelle."

"I think so, too!" I say. "I mean, they were actually on the boat. They must've seen something."

Cherry pulls her car keys from her purse and folds her arms. "I'm going to look into Mr. Pierson Mantelle. I don't even know where he lived. And what about his wife? I mean, he was on a boat with a twenty-year-old girlfriend. I'd say the wife would be a prime suspect. Do we even know if the police are looking at her?"

Annie shakes her head. "I wonder if his mother is still on the island. Did we figure out where Leigh Anne was staying?"

"His mother?" Cherry asks.

"Yeah," I say with an eye roll. "She showed up Wednesday evening when Craig and I were here after the police had left. The first time the police were here." I close my eyes at the police having been here more than once, then open them and finish. "She apparently grew up on the island. Lucy and Annie know her."

"*Knew* her," Annie emphasizes. "Leigh Anne Potts. Her mother still lives over on Beech Street, but we highly doubt she would stay with her. Lucy did find out she wasn't at The Isle."

Cherry looks around. "She came here? To your house? Why?"

"I, uh, I don't know. She was upset, and she didn't tell me at first that Pierson was her son. But something, oh… she called Craig C. J."

"What did he have to say about her? Did he remember her?" Tamela asks.

I half turn to look toward the porch where I sat after she left. I remember being folded over onto my knees and Craig leaving to go get dinner. And not coming home. "He, he didn't say anything." I keep my head low and don't look up at them. I'm tired. Tired of talking, tired of thinking, and really, really tired of seeing Craig through their eyes.

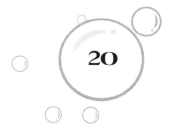

20

I've never been a scaredy-cat, like Tamela called herself earlier, but being in this huge house alone tonight, the thought of going to sleep isn't pleasant. This makes it easy to wait up for Craig. Plus, I did fix a big cup of coffee when the ladies left. Plus, I'm still pretty mad. Plus, I can't go to lunch with them tomorrow without some answers from my husband.

And I *really* want to go to lunch tomorrow.

It's ten thirty when I hear his car door close in the back drive. When he unlocks the back door, I'm standing in the hallway. He's wearing the casual clothes he's worn all day: shorts and a golf shirt with boat shoes. He's carrying a small laptop under his arm.

"Jewel? What is it?"

"Where have you been? I put the pizza in,

183

and by the time it was done you were gone. You didn't answer my texts or calls."

He turns into his office, so I follow him. He's not getting out of my sight this time.

"I needed to go out. Did you need me for something?" After laying his laptop on his desk, he turns and leans against the desk, looking at me.

"Yes. We need to talk, and I—" He holds up his hand to stop me, but I just take a breath and talk louder. "I don't care if you need to get some work done or whatever. We need—"

He brushes past me out the door, finishing my sentence. "To talk. Yes, we need to talk. I'm getting a glass of water. Can I get you anything?"

It's a little strange, but I am *not* leaving his side. I follow him into the kitchen and act like I can't decide what I want. I grab a glass out of the cabinet after him, fill it with ice after him, and then he fills it with water when he finishes filling his.

In the light from the refrigerator dispenser I look at him, and he looks sad, really sad. And tired. Our counselor, Dr. Kahill, said one of our problems is that we both have almost too much compassion. We are so careful to never hurt anyone, including each other, that we have lost ourselves. She said it would be like trying to have a relationship if we were each inside our own clear beach ball—never touching, never being honest, never really connecting at all for fear of hurting the other person. I close my eyes and mind to his weariness. I have to get through to him.

He motions for me to go ahead of him into the living room. I sit on the couch where I'd been earlier, and he settles into the chair across from me with a sigh. I ask, "That laptop you were carrying just now, is that yours?"

"Yes. It's the one I bought last summer, you remember? We bought it down at the mall, then went to dinner at Red Lobster so we could have those biscuits?" He smiles and looks around. "Who knew we'd be living by the ocean and eating seafood all the time in less than a year?" His smile dims, and he bends forward to set his glass of water on the floor beside him. Looking at the floor he mumbles, "But all the seafood in the world doesn't make up for all of this. Guess I was right all along about not moving here." Then he flops back in his chair and looks at the ceiling. "Pierson Mantelle. You know I didn't go to the marina that day looking for you to have lunch." He looks at me. "Did you tell the police that?"

"Me? No, but the ladies at lunch all knew that you didn't know where I was having lunch, so… they might've said it. Why were you meeting him? Who is he to you?"

"Some kind of cousin. I never really cared about any of this family stuff. You know I didn't. My mom didn't. But when we decided to take this house, I guess we should've expected some family drama. " He stares at me. "Right?"

A flush of heat makes me stir and lift my glass to my cheek. "Yes. You're right. We should've expected that, but…" But… I didn't know about your family? But… I didn't want to consider any negatives? But… for once I just wanted my way? But… With a wave of my hand, I finish the sentence by saying, "Whatever." I clear my throat and push the guilt away. I have questions I need answered; how we ended up here I know all too well.

"So, this Pierson," I say. "Did you talk to him that day? At the marina?"

Craig takes a breath and moves back in his seat. Finally he says, "The inheritance. It's not as straightforward as it seemed. You've heard about all the marina stuff, selling it to a private owner and all?"

"Yes, but what does that have to do with us?"

"Exactly!" He stands up, sinks his hands in his pockets, and starts walking around the room. "Pierson wanted to meet me on the boat that day. He'd sent me a couple emails before we moved, wanting to talk, but I was busy and I really didn't want to connect with any of the family. My mother always said they were manipulative and backstabbing. But once we were here, he said he had a business venture and so we met."

"On his boat that day?"

Craig stops his pacing in front of me. "We met a couple times before then."

"What? Why?"

"He was an important guy in the area, more in the central part of the state, but the company he was representing is huge and growing bigger. We were talking about a job."

"A job for you?"

"You know I've never bothered you with my work stuff. I like to keep work and family separate, and you seem to like it that way, too. I know Dr. Kahill thought we had too many separations in our lives, but I don't exactly agree. And now, it seems even less important that we share every little detail. You've got to know by now that's just not who I am."

I throw the pillow he slept on away from me, to the other end of the couch. I'd tucked it and his blanket behind the couch before the ladies came last night. A wave of embarrassment hits me as I think of them eating pizza and drinking wine on his 'bed.' I shout, "Except look at us! We have no idea what the other one is even doing! We're farther apart than ever!"

He jerks at my raised voice, then looks around the room and shrugs. "Point taken. Anyway, that last project I was on was going so badly that it really soured me on the company, and as you know, I was ready to dump it all and retire. However… "

"I know," I say. "This project in South Florida is a once-in-a-lifetime chance to really work on something big."

"And who wants to go out when you're on the bottom?" He picks up the pillow I just threw and sits down on that end of the couch. "Well, all that got me thinking, really thinking about the job Pierson suggested. It would've been a really big deal. More money, lots of control, and right here on Sophia Island. We could work on our marriage like you planned."

"Here? What, were you going to be the manager of the marina or something?" I grin because this all sounds made up.

My grin dies as he says, "Something like that. We hadn't really hashed out the details, but we were ready to. Plus, my background in environmental engineering was going to help pave the way with the locals."

Silly me, of course he didn't make it up; he doesn't think that far out of the box. I shake my head at his logical, confident demeanor. I can't get distracted. "Did you meet Pierson Mantelle on his boat the day he died?" All this other talk is making my head spin. I can't give into that and walk away from this conversation without my questions answered.

He seems to be examining the pillow in his hands, but when he looks up, his face is crunched in confusion. "Is this still about his murder? That has nothing to do with me." His confusion quickly softens into sadness, and his voice lowers. "But, no. No, Jewel, I didn't have a meeting with him that day on his boat. "

"Why not? If this job he was offering was so amazing?" I stop my question there. For some reason I want to cry. My eyes are watering, and my throat feels thick and rough. With some deep breaths, I try to loosen my chest and calm my sick stomach.

He is still playing with the pillow. Then he lays it on the couch between us. "Because I decided I didn't want the job here." His voice is solid, sure, and strange. Strange to me. "It only took a few days back here to know I can't live here. This house. This town. I can't do it."

"This wife?"

"I didn't say that. But Jewel…"

"I know. You were done with your wife back in Illinois. Why would it be different here? I just hoped… I don't know what I hoped, but I'm sorry. You were right; we should've never come here."

We sit and let time slip around us. Finally I stand up, collecting my still-full glass of water, my coffee cup, and my phone. "I'm tired. I'm going to bed." After a stop in the kitchen, I pause at the bottom of the front stairs. "Whatever you have to do to sell this place, go ahead. Then we can figure the rest out."

I'm on the third stair when he says my name. "Jewel, it's not that easy. Um, the inheritance? Well, it says we can't sell for five years."

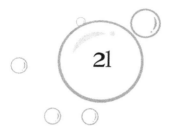

21

Of course I went back down those three steps last night. I was suddenly wide awake. We talked for almost another hour, but a lot of it went round in those same old circles. I'm beginning to see why we stopped talking years ago. Neither one of us is very good at it.

When I finally crawled into bed my brain switched off, and I fell into a deep sleep. Now it's four thirty in the morning, and I'm awake. Craig slept downstairs again, so I pulled the cover off our bed and am cuddled with it on a chair in our room looking out at the dark. The decorative streetlights are far away from the house itself, and the street looks like a scene in an old painting: pools of light on the narrow street, shadows caused by the thick moss, still air absorbing the circle of light.

When Craig said we were stuck here for five years, my first reaction was to laugh. We? We aren't stuck; it's your inheritance. You're stuck. Maybe I'd move to St. Louis and be near Erin and her sweet little family. Maybe I'd take some time and travel. Maybe I'd even move to Wisconsin to be near the boys in school, rent an apartment until they graduate. The speed with which these options appeared in my mind told me I'd been thinking up escape plans for a while, but they disappeared just as quickly when my husband reminded me of the papers *we'd* signed. We'd moved so often that we didn't come close to having a paid-off house; plus, housing in Chicagoland continually goes up in price. So, we'd taken out a loan, using this house as collateral, to pay for moving and provide money for any renovations here.

I know now that it was stupid for me to not pay more attention at the time, but I honestly thought this move was the answer to saving my marriage. I also didn't want to give Craig any reason to say no. I've never pushed him on anything, but I did on this and that might've been the death blow to our marriage. It was dying like a candle flame from lack of oxygen, but this move was like throwing a bucket of water at it.

It was some consolation last night when

Craig said he completely blamed himself, which was why he'd been secretly trying to figure a way out. Part of his deal with Pierson had been for Pierson to take over this house in exchange for the new job and a condo in the new complex that was going to be built at the marina. Craig said the bigger paycheck would let us pay off our loans quickly, and Pierson moving in would mean no renovation costs.

I jot down *condos at the marina* on the notepad I've got beside me. When I woke up with my mind swirling, I decided I need to try making some notes again. Condos at the marina would mean a big change for the waterfront. Until tonight I'd not heard anyone mention them.

When I asked about the break-in, Craig started in his circles again. He might know what it was about, but maybe it was just a teenager. He was also vague about the laptop. He couldn't figure out what I wanted to know about it.

I'd finally yelled, "Did someone break into our house to steal your personal laptop?"

After looking offended at my yelling, he shook his head and said, "I highly doubt it. People in small towns like this get all worked up when someone wants to change anything. Could someone think I know more about the marina purchase than I do and attempt to find out what I know by breaking into our home? Of course that's a possibility, but doesn't it seem a bit farfetched?"

That's when I gave up and went to bed.

As I look out the window, the details of the trees and the yard are becoming clearer as the darkness fades. A flush of anger pushes over me. It feels almost like a hot flash, except I'm not hot, just mad. I think I could like living here, maybe not in this ridiculous house, but here on Sophia Island. I like the ladies from last night. There's the beach, the river. I would enjoy living near my kids, but I really don't think that would work out in the long run. I'm not ready to just settle into being Grandma. Who would've ever guessed I'd feel this young when my kids were gone? So now what?

It felt so proactive when I wanted to move here. A new adventure. Dr. Kahill kept telling us we were taking our same issues with us. That thought drains away some of my anger, leaving a lot of hopelessness behind. She tried to warn us.

Okay. I sit up, pushing and kicking the blanket to the floor. First things first, this murder has to be solved, despite Craig's obtuse belief it has nothing to do with him. Whoever solves it, the police, Annie, I don't care, but as long as it's hanging over us we can't do anything else.

Sipping a small glass of orange juice, I stand for a moment at Craig's office door. I know he's in there, but for the life of me I can't force myself to even knock. I don't have anything to say to him right now. Before the sun was up, I was out walking around downtown and enjoyed watching the sun light up the island. That's another thing we keep meaning to do, a beach sunrise. Craig was off the couch and in our shower by the time I got home from my walk, but then I went straight to the basement to do laundry. Later, while I showered and changed, he made his coffee and ate, then closed himself in his office. Our paths throughout the house crossed a lot this morning, but we were never in the same room at the same time.

And here I stand. It's still hard to believe he doesn't realize he is truly in danger of being arrested for Pierson Mantelle's murder. Lying about being at the scene and lying about their relationship puts him at the top of the suspect list, but since he sees it as illogical, he thinks everyone sees it as illogical.

Whatever. I turn back to the kitchen. I cannot get into one of our conversations again this morning. Plus I'm not sure he would see something like being a murder suspect as important as his job. Friday is still a workday.

Out the front door, headed for my car, I breathe deeply of the salty, sandy, musty old town. I swing my arms, which makes my jacket sleeves swing, too. This makes me smile. This is the first outfit I bought after moving here, and this is my first time wearing it: gauzy cotton pants with wide legs and a funky, pink seashell trim on the bottoms. The pants and jacket are soft green, accented with gray swirls that look like waves. The sleeveless shirt is seashell pink to match the trim. My gray flip-flops have shiny stones on them, and my hair is up in a clip, which also has shiny stones on it. I bought it all on an impulse when I truly believed Craig and I were going to be happy here. I've been saving it for a special day out together.

Oh well.

I turn my car around in the circle drive and pull out, headed for the library. The library is within walking distance but the beach isn't, and I don't want to come home in between.

Two matters are taking me to the library. One – researching the marina not only here, but marinas around the state. It seems like that is at the bottom of Pierson being here and is what

has the greatest number of people upset. Two —
I'm here for a mystery.

The kind that comes in a book.

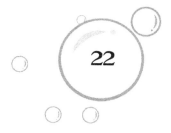

22

When I walk out of the library the bright sunlight makes me shut my eyes tight. I blink until they adjust. This reminds me of being a college student after an extended study session.

Another feeling comes over me from those college days: I'm responsible for no one. Usually with Craig home I'd be thinking of how to make him happy, constantly wondering what he might need. What does he want for dinner? For lunch? Does he need shirts from the dry cleaner's? All that seems to have just dissipated. The day is mine. There's no one I feel I want to keep happy, check up on, or even feed. Just a Friday with me and my friends. I've only walked half a block when I stop to take off the thin jacket I'd appreciated inside the chilly library. I fold it and put it in my big canvas bag along with my books. Yes, books. The ladies told me a couple of authors to look up and even the names of the first books in their mystery series. I ended up with *Catering to Nobody* by Diane Mott Davidson and *Death on Demand* by Carolyn Hart. I was shocked at how many books are in each of those series—the ladies last night said they'd read them all!

With my bag back on my shoulder, I turn through the parking lot behind the library. On the other side I cross the street in front of some delightfully small restaurants, one with a wooden pirate ship for children to play on. I turn to the left and walk into an adorable bakery I've noticed but never stopped in. I'd texted the ladies first thing this morning that I'd bring dessert to lunch.

Soft colors, soft smells, soft icing, and beautiful cakes make me want to swoon.

"Welcome to Karen's. Can I help you?" a voice says, attempting to pull my attention from the case of delightful offerings.

"Yes," I say, finally looking up.

The lady is older than me, but the most striking thing about her is how happy she looks. She laughs as she wipes her hands on her apron. "I like someone who knows they need help."

"Well, I just know I need dessert for lunch

today, and I'm not leaving here without it. What do you suggest?"

"Oh, an assortment of cupcakes is always popular. Especially since I just finished this beach trio: coconut fudge, cherry limeade, and piña colada." She points to a plate of cupcakes, all iced in bright colors with seashell decorations.

"I'll take, oh, give me a dozen. The hostess apparently loves sweets, so I can leave her some."

"A dozen it is. Are you new here?"

"I am. My name is Jewel." She notices how I choke off before I say my last name, but she doesn't look too curious, just keeps boxing up my treats.

"I'm Karen, nice to meet you."

"Karen, as in the owner of Karen's Bakery?"

"Yes, that's me. Started in my house four years ago and just moved into this place last year. It's all a dream come true." Her hair is gray and cut short. She's medium height and a bit heavy. Actually, she looks like a grandma. She just makes you want to smile.

"That's nice, your dream coming true." I can't help but sigh, and again, she notices with a quick glance in my direction.

She ties a pretty lilac ribbon around the box, then writes up my bill. After being so friendly and open, she now seems focused only on her duties: running my card, making sure the box is closed properly, then handing me the cupcakes and helping me maneuver out the door. It's almost like she's hurrying me out, and even more so when she closes the door behind me with a clipped goodbye.

I'm on the sidewalk, a tad confused, when the door is yanked back open and my name is practically shouted. "Jewel! Oh, you're still right here." Karen steps out and lays a hand on my arm. "Honey, I'm sorry, but sometimes I get these feelings so strong about people that I should say something to them. Now that I have this business I try to not do it with strangers, but well, honey, I just feel like I have to tell you something."

She's looking up at me with such bright gray eyes, full of fire. She's practically bouncing in place with whatever she wants to say, so I brace myself and nod. "Sure. What is it?"

As her smile widens, her body relaxes, her eyes soften, and she says, "Don't give up on happiness." She steps away from me. "That's all. Don't give up on happiness. Now you have a good day."

Like a postman walking away from a door he's just made a big delivery to, she fairly struts back into her bakery and leaves me staring after her. I don't have a free hand to open the door, but the words are already forming in my mouth to ask what she means. She said she'd told me all she had to say. I guess I'll have to stop in again. Soon.

"Karen is a doll. These will be the best cupcakes you've ever eaten in your life!" Tamela says as she holds the door open for me at Lucy's mother's home. The house is one of the older ones along this stretch of the beach, but it looks to be in good repair. The driveway goes underneath the house, and there's room for parking there. The door Tamela is holding open is from the parking area up a set of interior stairs. We come out onto a narrow deck on the side of the house. She holds that door, too, as she steps out before me, then moves to the side.

"Just go on down to the back deck," she says, so I lead the way down the side of the house, with a worn wood railing on one side of me and a wall of long, narrow windows on the other. At the end of the house, the deck opens up to a view of the dunes and the ocean. Waves crash, and I'm arrested by the idea of living here. Being able to see the ocean any time? Why, I never even imagined this.

"Hey, did you forget about me?" Tamela says since my stopping trapped her on the walkway part of the deck.

"Oh, sorry. This is amazing. I guess I never thought of people actually living on the beach."

Tamela has stepped around me to knock on the sliding glass door. "There's Birdie," she says as she slides it open, and I leave the view to meet our host.

"Oh, Tamela, you're as pretty as ever. Being retired agrees with you!" the little woman says as she opens the door. She hugs Tamela, then turns to me. Her bright face folds in a bit. "Do I know you?"

"Oh, no, you don't. I'm Jewel Mantelle. We're new here."

Her face folds in even more. "But, but I know Mantelles. Don't I, Tamela?"

Tamela smiles at her and gives me a quick side glance. "Yes, ma'am, you do. Let's take the cupcakes inside. Jewel is married to one of the Mantelles from here, and they just moved back. Oh, it feels so nice inside out of the sun. Can't believe it's already gotten so warm this year." She has guided us inside and pointed me to the kitchen, although with the open floorplan, I'd already spotted it. "Miss Birdie, Lucy will be here with lunch any minute. Annie's coming, too."

"Come talk to me, Mrs. Mantelle," our host says. "I love meeting new people."

"You have such a beautiful home. I can hardly imagine living right on the beach like this." I reach out my hand to her. "Now that I've set down that box I can meet you properly. I'm Jewel," I say, taking a seat on the couch next to her chair.

"Yes, that's right. Jewel. What a pretty name. Is it like jewels in a necklace or short for Julia?"

"Jewels in a necklace."

She laughs and puts her hands together in a clap. "I thought so. So which of the Mantelle boys did you marry? When we were newly here you couldn't throw a rock without hitting a Mantelle. Not so much anymore."

"My husband is Craig, and he only stayed here in the summers with his aunt. His great-aunt, really, I guess. Everyone called him C. J."

"Oh," she says as she sits back. Her eyes shift to look out at the windows. I follow her lead and look at the waves, but suddenly she blurts, "He stayed in the big house? With Corabelle?"

"Yes. His mother worked up in Atlanta where he lived the rest of the year. Did you know his aunt?"

She's blinking at me. It's like watching that spinning wheel when my tablet is taking its time to load. Then her words slowly unravel. "You inherited the big house downtown? Oh my, I don't leave my perch here by the sea often, but I would for a look at your home. How many times I walked or drove past it! Even while Cora-belle was still there, I wondered just what it was like. Can I come see it?"

"Why, of course! The ladies were all there last night."

Tamela has joined us. "It's pretty cool, Miss Birdie, but I guess I expected it to be scarier or something. Maybe haunted? It's pretty much just a big old house plumb stuffed with furni-ture."

The older lady's eyes are more sure and her speech more steady now that she's connected with the correct memories. "When we moved here in 1968 some of the big houses downtown had been sold or were falling apart. Only a few were still in the hands of the original families, and those families stuck together. Sent their kids off to private schools or even had tutors for their children. Folks like us were never invited to the parties there. It felt like one of those living history museums to just walk in some of those neighborhoods. And there in the middle of it all was the biggest house, all closed up with an old lady living in it alone. Then when her nephew—my word, that was your husband—would come in the summer, she still never ventured out. It was strange to see him out and about and know he went back to that huge, dark house every night."

Tamela and I are staring at her like she's telling ghost stories around a campfire, so when Lucy comes sailing in the side door we both yelp.

"You liked to scared us to death!" Tamela says. We jump up to help Lucy with her things.

"Annie's right behind me. You won't believe what she's brought." Lucy rolls her eyes and shakes her head at us.

"Someone get this door!" Annie hollers. "My hands are full, and I can't wait for Cherry."

I pull the door open wide, and in she comes, lumbering, carrying a huge glass pitcher full of yellow-green liquid.

"Limes and salt are in my bag. I figured having a pitcher of margaritas like Pierson Mantelle was beamed with will help our detecting!"

"Can't hurt, I guess," I say.

Cherry comes running up the stairs. "I feel so bad. I didn't even think to bring anything."

"From the looks of things I don't think we need anything else at all," Tamela says with a laugh.

Lucy is opening containers of salad and emptying her bags of crackers and chips. "Y'all want to have lunch outside? Start carrying all this out and I'll get the plates and utensils."

On the end of the back deck, across from the walkway we arrived on earlier, the deck is covered. A table for eight is tucked into the corner. With everyone working, the table is pulled away from the wall and set, the chair cushions brushed off and claimed, and margaritas poured in no time at all.

Birdie raises her glass. "I want to make the toast. To the ocean. To the sea. To having you all here with me!"

They'd given me the honored seat as a first-time guest, even though Cherry has never been here either apparently, and I'm looking directly at the beach. Even with the drama and the lack of sleep from last night, I can't help but be in a good amount of awe. I'm sitting on a deck overlooking the beach with new friends, sipping a margarita.

Annie grimaces at me, tips her glass in my direction, and says, "Drink up, friend. You're going to need it when you hear what I learned this morning about the murder."

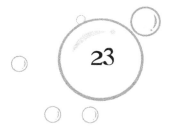

23

The squawks of the seagulls have nothing on us. Apparently we'd all taken our assignments from Lucy seriously last night, and we all wanted to tell what we'd discovered first. Finally Cherry half stands from her low seat, holding her long arms out over the table.

"Stop! I can't hear what everyone is saying, and we're going to give our hostess a stroke with all this. Now, who thinks they should go first?" Cherry's short, dark hair is still wet from the shower she told us she took after her morning run on the beach. Her arms are muscular, as her legs must also be to hold that stance for as long as she is. With a nod at Annie's raised hand, Cherry pulls her arms in and plops back down in her seat. "Annie has the floor."

"Thank you for having us here, Lucy and

Miss Birdie." Annie looks around the table as we all lift our just-refilled glasses. We take sips and carefully set our glasses back down.

"These are very good, Annie," Lucy says. "Tasty but not too strong."

Annie beams. "I do make a good margarita. Oh, maybe we should've toasted Pierson's memory? Although I don't guess we have many memories of him, do we? He was quite a bit younger than most of us."

That spreads a pall over the table; then Annie shakes her head and clears her throat. "Which is another reason we have to help figure this out. So, sorry, Jewel, but Craig is back up near the top of the police suspect list. They found out about the dockominiums."

"The what?" the ladies ask.

Annie responds quickly. "Dockominiums are what they call condominiums on the dock, or at least in the dock area. You buy a boat slip at the dock when you buy your condominium. I'd never heard the term either, but I bet we'll be hearing it a lot more in the future," she says with a knowing look.

Tamela shakes her head as she takes a forkful of chunky crab salad. She hides her mouth with her hand as she asks, "Here? Where in the world would there be room to put condos near the dock?"

"Annie's right," I say as I lift my glass for another drink. "Craig and Pierson were going to be partners in this whole scheme."

"What!" Lucy exclaims. "They knew each other?" She turns to Annie. "And what is this about condos at the marina? I mean, there was some pipe-dream plan a few years back, but it was unworkable with the city owning the marina."

"That's why Pierson's company wanted to own the marina," Annie explains. "They've done it a lot down south apparently. The police interviewed Adam. You remember my oldest son, Adam, Miss Birdie? He works down at the marina."

Miss Birdie is fading on us, so she lightly smiles and nods at Annie.

"Anyway," Annie continues, "Adam was fit to be tied to find out they were making all these plans behind the scenes. His friends from down south at marinas that have gone from public to private have different opinions on how it worked out. Some good, some not so good. However, any that were bought by the company Pierson was representing turned out bad. Awful, as a matter of fact. They misled the communities about how much access they'd have to the slips and priced the ones not associated with the doc-kominiums out of sight. He's heard of slips, just a slip with no condo, being bought for well over one hundred thousand dollars!"

Lucy's shoulders fall. "That's a lot of money for politicians to ignore." We all agree, then take a moment to eat and drink as the wind has been taken right out of our sails.

Cherry folds her napkin and lays it on her plate. "But you said Craig works with building roads. How would he be working with Pierson Mantelle and the whole marina thing at all?"

They all are looking at me. Dr. Kahill always encouraged me to make friends. My kids say I need friends. I actually have wanted friends. It's just not that easy for me to share, to talk about what's going on in my life, but this keeping everything to myself, keeping all my thoughts private, feels crazier and crazier, especially now that the idea of me and Craig growing closer is obviously a delusion. I sit up straighter and take another sip of margarita.

"Margaritas were a good idea, Annie. Thanks." I take a deep breath. "Okay, here goes. Craig was involved with Pierson because the in-heritance on the house has us tied to it for the next five years." I ignore the looks around the table and the intakes of breath. "Craig was trading the house to Pierson for the marina manager's job and a condominium in the new complex. I didn't hear the term dockominiums, but that sounds about right. I never knew any of this."

"But…" Tamela's words come slowly. "But if they were partners, what motive would Craig have to, uh, you know?"

"Pierson had promised the manager position to someone else, too," Annie says. "Ray Barnette. Ray is right in the thick of all this, so I guess he would've been competition for Craig." She's studying her plate and not looking at me.

"But Craig says he'd decided he didn't want the job," I blurt out. "Decided he doesn't want to be here all the time." At the suspicious looks around the table, I nod and say, "I know. Maybe he's lying about that, but I don't think so." I lift my glass, ready for another sip as I mumble, barely loud enough for them to hear, "I think he's done with everything on Sophia Island. Especially his wife."

No one argues with me.

After a pause, Annie says, "Well, Ray was up to his neck in this thing. More so than he let on at first, but there's more…"

Miss Birdie has fallen asleep, and a little snore from her causes Annie to lower her voice.

"Sheryl-Lee was working with another company that's in competition with the one Pierson worked for. She's been trying like everything to get a copy of the plan Pierson was working from. Allie, y'all remember my daughter Allie and Sheryl-Lee have been best friends forever? You met them both, Jewel. Well, Allie's grown pretty jealous of Sheryl-Lee. Last night after dinner she told me Sheryl-Lee had been sleeping with Pierson to find out his plan!"

"Oh my," Lucy says. "You see that kind of thing in movies, but would a man who has two twenty-year-olds on his boat be so smitten with Sheryl-Lee King he'd tell her his secrets?"

Cherry laughs. "Oh, I think it's more that she would have access to his papers and things. Not that he'd be doing any pillow talk." We all nod and take a minute to think. Cherry continues. "On the girlfriend front, I found out the police have not talked to either of the girls except through their lawyer. They didn't return to college; they both went home. The girlfriend is from California, and her mother is some big lawyer out there. She's apparently shut down any and all lines of questioning. One of my friends is a nurse at another private school, and she said she's not surprised that they are protecting their students. She said most of the parents there are important people who know how to use, or ignore, the system."

Lucy throws her napkin onto her plate. "But they were on a boat when a man was killed! How can they just refuse to talk to the police?"

Tamela motions for Lucy to keep her voice down, but Lucy smiles at her sleeping mother. "No worry, she's out for a while. Matter of fact, she'll be so upset she missed our conversation, I'll have to relay it all to her tonight. But I'm serious, what are the police going to do? Those girls were right there!"

Annie sighs. "Remember, the police don't think it could be either of the girls because they were too drunk and too weak."

Lucy scoots her chair out to face the beach and slouches further down in her seat. "We'll clean all this up in a minute and have our dessert, but right now this is just too comfortable." The rest of us move our seats to face the waves as well.

Annie divides the rest of the margarita pitcher among our glasses. "There, you get the most, Jewel. Sounds like it wasn't a fun conversation with your husband last night."

This time when I start to speak it's not nearly as hard. Maybe it's due to the margarita, maybe the sunshine, maybe the sound of the waves, but whatever it is, my lips are loose. "No, it wasn't fun. He hates it here. Doesn't want to stay here—no, says he *won't* stay here. Or at least won't stay in the house. I completely understand why he's at the top of the suspects list, not that I think he did it, but he's so oblivious to how all of this looks. He's such a nuts-and-bolts guy, a true engineer. Exactly who you want building bridges and airplanes, but he has no sense of the big picture. Also, he can't lie to save his life." I laugh and then grimace. "He can't even pull a practical joke. There's no way he could face a police interrogation and tell a plausible, made-up story. Just no way."

Laying my head back and closing my eyes, I lift my arms in a shrug before letting them fall limply at the sides of my chair.

No one says anything for a moment, and I'm actually so relaxed I may have started to doze off. Then Tamela clears her throat. "I taught school for a lot of years. I remember many kids like your husband, honest to a fault. Didn't have a clue how to lie."

"Exactly," I slur. Hearing my slur, I sit up and smile as I shake my head to wake up. "Think I was dozing off."

Tamela smiles at me, but I feel a tension be-hind her smile. She leans toward me from across the table. "The only problem with those kinds of people is they can lie if forced into a corner. It may not be comfortable for them, but it's not impossible. I had that happen with a student I went way out on a limb for because I just knew he couldn't be lying."

Now I'm awake. "Do you think Craig is lying?"

"Oh, sweetie, I don't know. I just don't want you to get too far out on a limb like I did." She settles back in her chair, still looking troubled.

Lucy also looks troubled as she reminds me, "He's already lied a couple times, right? About not being at the marina, not knowing Pierson Mantelle, the inheritance…"

Annie's frown deepens. "And about knowing you were there at the marina that day for lunch. Sorry, but I did have to tell Aiden that. He said they'd already heard it from one of the other ladies from our lunch group."

"Yeah." I smile at her. "I figured. Okay, Craig's on the top of the list. Who else besides the college girls is also on the list?"

Cherry points at Tamela. "Do you still have your notebook?"

Tamela pulls it out of her seat. "Right here. What else did you find out from Ray, Annie?"

Annie's defensive. "Why do you think I talked to Ray? Maybe I got everything from Adam."

"Maybe," Tamela says, tapping her pen against her chin. "But then what were you and Ray talking about at Antonio's late last night?"

Like toddlers hearing the rattle of a cookie bag, all of our heads swing to look at Annie.

"Leaving Jewel's house last night, I ran into him and we went for a quick drink. That's all. I was investigating." Her big, blue eyes flash at us. "That's all."

Tamela shrugs. "Sounded like it was pretty cozy. Antonio's can be pretty dark and the drinks pretty strong."

Annie is blushing. She looks down at the table. "We're old friends. Besides, I felt sorry for him, trying to get around on that old pair of crutches."

"Crutches?" Lucy asks.

"He sprained his ankle. Had it all wrapped up."

"Poor man," I say. "Being a janitor is hard enough. I bet he's on his feet all day. Hopefully he won't lose his job. He said he really needed it."

Now heads swivel toward me, but I'm the only one still looking concerned. "What?"

Cherry laughs. "Oh, I never did fill you in

on Mr. Barnette, did I? Ray Barnette can't lose his job unless he fires himself. He owns Plantation Services, the largest cleaning, sanitation, and whatever-else-they-do company in the whole region. They have the contract for most of the hotels and businesses. Even have the local government contract."

"Then why was he cleaning the offices at town hall that day?"

Annie throws up a hand. "He started the company being a janitor, so he fills in occasionally just to see how things are going. He did get kind of agitated when I asked him what his new job would've been like with the marina." Her scowl deepens. "He said he'd found out Pierson was double-dealing him and he was glad he was dead. But you know, what if Ray was this angry before Pierson died?"

Cherry tilts her head and studies Annie. "How did he hurt his foot? You said he was on crutches?"

Annie shakes her head. "He never really did say. Probably stepped off a curb wrong."

Cherry clasps her hands in front of her mouth and thinks for a moment. "Or could he have hurt it falling out of a first-floor window when he was surprised during his search of his competition's office?"

Lucy gasps. "At Jewel's house! The police said it looked like the person fell leaving, didn't they?"

I hit my forehead with the palm of my hand. "I forgot to tell you. Craig does have another laptop for personal business. He had it with him last night when he got home. He seemed completely stumped as to why I was asking him about it. However, he did admit someone could've broken in to get the plans for the marina from him. Someone against the marina, not in competition for his job. I wonder if he even knows he had competition. Anyway, he had it with him last night, so I guess no one got it."

Annie's voice drops to a low rumble as she points at me. "I said I ran into Ray last night? Well, he was at the end of your street, walking. He had a small canvas bag over his shoulder, and when he got in the car I saw it was empty so I asked him what it was for. He said he'd needed to bring 'something back to someone,' and he had to carry it in the bag since he was on crutches."

"I just got chills," Lucy says. "What if he was bringing Craig's laptop back to him?"

We are all staring at each other. Apparently Lucy isn't the only one with chills. We all jump and yelp when Miss Birdie pipes up, "Did I miss dessert?"

Once the shock is over, we laugh and begin clearing the table. I deliver a stack of dishes to the kitchen and open the box of cupcakes. It smells like Karen's bakery, and as much as I'm looking forward to a cupcake, my main feeling at the moment is aggravation.

Nothing diminishes the pleasure of a freshly baked cupcake decorated with a glorious pile of frosting like realizing your husband might be so obtuse he's going to end up in jail.

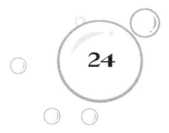

24

"Let's have dessert inside," Lucy says as she comes in off the deck. "I'm making a pot of coffee, but there's also water and iced tea in the fridge. Help yourselves."

Cherry had walked in with Miss Birdie on her arm, and they are looking at the collection of pictures on the far wall. I join them as the small kitchen fills with the others cleaning up. I deliver the cupcakes to the coffee table, then step over to the wall of pictures. Miss Birdie takes hold of my arm as I get close.

"Come look at my pictures. You girls won't believe how much fun we had here back in those days. We drove all over the beach and had fires at night. Mr. Fellows, Lucy's father, loved to fish. All the pictures of him and his fish are on the other wall over there. Cherry, where did you move here from?"

"The Atlanta area. Our kids were grown, and my husband's company asked if we wanted to relocate to Jacksonville. We were delighted to find it was an easy commute to his office from here. We'd vacationed here years ago and loved it."

"Oh my," Miss Birdie says. "He drives all the way to Jacksonville every day?"

"Not anymore. He changed jobs recently and works from home, but after years of Atlanta traffic a thirty-five-minute commute with comparatively little traffic was nothing to him. I still work at the hospital on the island, but only on weekends. I'm a nurse."

Miss Birdie grins and squeezes Cherry's arm with hers. "I just love nurses! They make being in the hospital almost fun, don't you think?"

We laugh and are pulled along by the older woman. She makes a motion with her head at another section of pictures. "See here, Jewel, there are some of the old houses downtown. I don't believe your home is in any of these. Most were taken at the parades or during home tours… no, I don't see the Mantelle house. Remember, you promised to let me in to see it, right?"

"Yes, ma'am, I did."

She lets go of Cherry's arm and turns fully toward me. "I know it looked like I slept through everything that was said out there during lunch, but I heard some things." She lifts her free hand to touch my cheek. "I hope you stay here, Jewel Mantelle. That family, and this island, is lucky to have you—now act like it!" She grins and pinches my cheek.

"Ow," I say with a laugh. "It's been a long time since I've had my cheek pinched." Bending over to hug her, I whisper, "Thank you. I'll remember that. Want a cupcake?"

She pulls away. "Just one? That's an awfully large box. I bet my daughter told you I have a sweet tooth. Let's go sit down."

Once she's seated, I walk into the kitchen and pour myself a cup of coffee. Back in the living room, Tamela is already scribbling in her notepad. "Okay, people we're still checking on that are involved some way are Craig Mantelle, Ray Barnette, Sheryl-Lee King, the girlfriend and her friend. Wait, what about Pierson's wife? Weren't we going to check on her?"

"I did. Just a minute." Lucy is bent over the coffee table cutting one of the coconut fudge cupcakes in half. "I want to try one of the other flavors in a minute," she says as she puts the half on her plate and sits down. "Okay, I knew his mother played tennis with a friend of mine in Ponte Vedra, so I called Paula and talked to her this morning." She flips back in her book to a previous page. "Turns out Pierson's wife also plays in that league. Her name is… here it is, Saundra. She checked and found out both Leigh Anne and Saundra canceled practices for this week. Apparently the two of them are pretty tight. I actually got both of their cell numbers." She looks up, then around the circle of us. "Can anyone think of a reason why we should call them?"

We all focus on our cupcakes as we think. Cherry says, "I don't think we're doing this detective thing right. Feels too muddled, don't you think?"

Annie speaks with her mouth full of chocolate. "Not that many murders for us to practice on, you know."

"That's a good thing, right?" I say. They all nod, but I'm not sure they're being sincere. After all, none of their husbands are at the middle of the case.

Miss Birdie had excused herself while we were talking. Now she comes out of the door on the left side of the room. She leaves the door open, and we can see a large bedroom behind it. She has put on a lightweight peach cardigan that matches her outfit, and her purse is hanging from her arm.

Pointing at the table, she instructs her daughter. "Pack up a half dozen of those cupcakes. Mimi Potts is expecting us."

Lucy stands up. "Mimi Potts, Leigh Anne's mother?"

"Yes. Isn't that a good place for us to get some answers about Pierson's family? I called Mimi, expressing my condolences on the death of her grandson. Told her I wanted to stop by with some friends. Girls, are you coming with me? If you are, then you need to shake a leg!"

Cherry and Tamela begged off as they had plans for the afternoon. I tried to get out of going since I don't know the poor woman and I'm not really good in situations like this. I never know what to say. However, Miss Birdie said I was most definitely going to pay my respects as I was practically family to her friend. She also said something about me needing to learn what it meant to be Southern. Plus, she pointed out that I'd bought the cupcakes.

So here I am walking up the pine straw–stained sidewalk toward a small, rundown ranch house. We'd arrived in two cars and parked out by the road, but there are no cars in the driveway, which surprised us all.

Annie whispers, "Wouldn't you think there would be more people here?"

"Maybe everyone came yesterday," Lucy says. "I haven't been in this neighborhood in years. It's looking a little worse for wear, isn't it?"

"It's not in the best area, and it never was very nice," Annie says. "Some of the houses look abandoned, but some look like folks are working on them. Amber says you can get a good deal in this area if you're willing to do some renovation."

Lucy rings the doorbell, and we listen to see if it works. After a second push with no accompanying sound, Lucy knocks on the crooked screen door. We hear a voice, and then the wooden door behind it is slowly pulled open. The little old woman on the other side is wearing a light pink housecoat, and her gray hair is cut short. She grins and pushes on the screen door. "Come in! Come in! Law, it's been ages, Birdie! Who are these pretty young women you've dragged to an old woman's door?"

"Mimi, it sure is good to see you again. Hate the circumstances, though," Birdie says as we all file in.

Mrs. Potts closes the door, which makes the

dark room even darker and the air more stale, if that's possible. She practically falls into a big, dark recliner and points Birdie to a matching chair beside her. The other three of us take the couch. Birdie tries to sit politely on the edge of the chair, but it sucks her in so that her feet are in the air, sticking straight out. Annie's eyes light up, and she looks like she's going to laugh right out loud.

Lucy nudges her with her elbow and clears her throat. "Momma, are you okay?"

"Sure am," she says as she arranges herself. "This is right comfortable, isn't it, Mimi?"

"Best thing since sliced bread," Mimi says, and then she points to the box I'm holding. "What's that?"

"Oh, some cupcakes. Would you like one? You don't know me, Mrs. Potts. I'm Jewel."

From the depths of her chair, Birdie speaks up. "Jewel *Mantelle*. She's married to that boy C. J. what would stay with Corabelle in the summers. Remember, Mimi? Jewel here just moved into the house."

"The Mantelle house? The big one?"

"Yes, ma'am. Can I get you a cupcake?"

"Oh me, oh my!" She cackles as she leans forward. Her chair leans with her so it looks like she might fall out. "Wait'll Leigh Anne finds out about you!"

I clear my throat and smile deciding to not say I've already had the pleasure of meeting her daughter. "I'm so sorry about your grandson, Mrs. Potts."

She sits back. "Yes, that is sad. But I ain't seen him in years, so…" She shrugs. "I will take one of them cupcakes. There are some paper plates in the kitchen if you don't mind."

Lucy and Annie leap up to help me with what is clearly a one-person job.

In the kitchen, we huddle around the small table, where we find a stack of paper plates and some other food offerings. Annie shakes her head, then yells, "Mrs. Potts, okay if we put some of this food in here away so it won't spoil?"

"I'd be obliged," the older lady yells back.

Lucy starts opening the cabinets looking for containers. "I told you Leigh Anne wouldn't be staying here. Think her mother even knows where she is? I wonder if she's already gone back home to Ponte Vedra."

Annie hands me a roll of Saran Wrap. "If she's not seen Pierson in years, she probably hasn't seen his wife either. This may not help our investigation, but at least we're doing a good deed."

"Things are really pretty clean in here. You think she has some help?" I ask as I look around at the worn appliances, torn linoleum, and faded paint.

"Possibly," Annie says.

I've decided on taking her a piña-colada cupcake, so I carry that out to Mimi on a paper plate. "Here you are. They're from Karen's Bakery and are delicious. Can I get you anything to drink with it?"

"No, hon. I still have some coffee. This is mighty nice of you. I wish my Leigh Anne were here. I know she'd love to meet you. She always dreamed of living in that house. When she was a girl she'd sit outside it for hours, just a-dreaming."

"I did get to meet her. She came by the house one day."

Mrs. Potts scowls. "Now she never told me that."

"Does she usually stay here with you when she visits?" The question is out of my mouth before I even know I've formed it.

With a light yellow frosting mustache, Mrs. Potts shakes her head. "No. She usually stays over at the Bellingtons'." She takes another big bite, and I back away with a smile.

"I'll go help them finish up." Bellingtons'? That sounds so familiar.

Annie and Lucy are waiting around the corner for me with excited grins. They pull me into the kitchen. Annie says, "You did good! You sounded just like a detective."

"Who are the Bellingtons? It sounds familiar."

"We were there Wednesday. Charlotte Bellington, remember? The inn her son and daughter-in-law run. They'd be around Leigh Anne's age; maybe they're friends."

Lucy looks around. "We're done in here. So now what?"

Annie says, "I need to get home and change for Florida Friday. Y'all going?"

"What is it?" I ask as we walk back into the living room.

"There's a live band on Centre Street. Everyone brings lawn chairs and hangs out. Sometimes we dance, but mostly we listen to the music and visit. Everybody goes."

"I'll check with Craig, but it's been a long week so we may just stay in." Craig being around does come in handy as an excuse when I need one.

We rush to help Miss Birdie out of her chair as she's pushing to sit up straight. When we've got her up and on her own two feet, she says to me, "Jewel girl, you listen to me. Don't wait on a man to have fun! Now, Mimi, it was good to see you. I hate that you didn't get the chance to be closer to your grandson, but it is what it is."

We are all heading out the door, having told Mrs. Potts to not get up. I'm pulling the screen door shut as she yells, "Hey, Mantelle lady! Can you get me another cupcake? That sure was good."

I tell the others I'll be right back. As I walk through the living room, I ask, "Chocolate fudge or cherry limeade?"

"Cherry limeade sounds good."

I bring it to her as she turns on the television. "Thank you, ma'am," she says. "You come visit me any time. I'll tell Leigh Anne you say hi. I'm sure she'll be back around to see you real soon. You and that house."

"Okay, um, sure," I say. This time I get both doors closed behind me. Everyone's in the cars. Birdie is with her daughter, and I see Annie is also in their car in the back seat.

"I can give you a ride, Annie."

"I know, but they've got to go practically by my front door. It's out of the way for you. See you tonight, right?"

I open my mouth, but catch Birdie's sharp

eye. "Okay. Maybe—no, not maybe. Yes. Whether Craig is interested or not, I'll try to be there."

Their car pulls out while I get in mine. I pull down the visor to block out the sun, which is hitting the windshield full on. I catch my reflection in the mirror on the back of the visor, meet my own eyes, and grimace. "You liar."

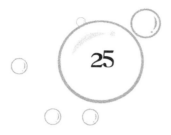

25

"Did your husband tell you he and I had another long talk this afternoon?" Officer Greyson asks when he gets to me. I'd seen him standing at the corner of the building on Centre, where he watched the Florida Friday crowd. I thought he also saw me, but I hoped not as I swerved off the sidewalk and into the crowd to avoid him. He cut me off as I tried to emerge from the unorganized jumble of lawn chairs, coolers, wagons, dogs, and people.

"Oh! Hello. Looks like a good crowd tonight," I say with a smile and a bit of a bounce. I changed into shorts, a T-shirt, and tennis shoes before leaving the house. My tennis shoes make me bounce like I want to run, but I don't really run. Some of the bounce may just be that I'm agitated. Very agitated.

Officer Greyson is tall, and I tilt my head up to look at him as he scans the crowd again. "Lots of folks enjoy it." He drops his head and stares at me. "Your husband joining you for the concert?"

"Uh, no. I'm not here for all that. No chair," I say with a lift of my hands. "Just out for a walk and thought I'd check it out. Better get going, let you get back to work."

But Officer Greyson is persistent. "I asked you if your husband told you about our conversation this afternoon. He said you were out with some friends. He didn't seem to know what friends or where you were. So, are you keeping secrets from him, or is he too preoccupied with the mess he's in to listen to you?"

Okay, neither of those is a good option. "He just forgot, I guess. Or, I don't know, maybe I didn't tell him." I try to turn down Centre Street, which is closed for the concert. All those lawn chairs have to sit somewhere. "Glad you got to talk to him."

He reaches out and brushes my arm. "Mrs. Mantelle, you need to understand things are getting ready to change."

I feel like a bucket of ice water has been dumped over me with his words. They're getting ready to arrest Craig. I can just feel it.

"Our lead investigator is cutting his vacation short and will be here tomorrow to take over this investigation. He's, well…" Officer Greyson drops his eyes from me and studies his shoes. "Let me put it this way." He's stepped closer, and his eyes are boring into mine. "He'll make an arrest by tomorrow night. I'm confident of that."

"But if you're confident of that, why aren't you making an arrest? Who's he going to arrest?"

"Probably your husband."

There, another bucket of ice water. This one's settling in my stomach. "Why? Do you really think Craig murdered that man?"

He scoffs and takes a step back. "Have I arrested him?" Then he leans toward me and whispers, "I'm trying to give you a heads-up that you and your husband need to get on the same page and realize this is not a joke. I don't think your husband is taking this seriously."

The bounce in my step dribbles away, and my earlier anxiety melts into exhaustion. "I agree, Officer Greyson. Craig is a one-track thinker. He knows what he knows and doesn't think it's logical for anyone to come to a different conclusion."

"All well and good until he runs up against someone that is basically illogical." He says this to me with waggling eyebrows, bugging eyes, and several throat clearings, leaving me to know that the inspector showing up tomorrow is the object of his warning.

Greyson steps back to watch the crowd around us. As I look up at him I make a decision. "I'm going to trust you."

He winks with a small smile. "Good move." He pauses, does another quick scan, then turns away from the crowd and dips his head toward me once more. "I'll prove it to you right now. I agree about your husband. I don't believe he thinks outside the box enough to commit murder. Just don't think it would register in his brain. I see it when I talk to him. However, he's not being completely forthright about some things, and I'm not sure what that's all about. That's what he needs to clear up and get off the table. He can't give Detective Johnson anything to grab on to. I mean, we all know your husband's lying, right?"

I grimace but then nod.

"We don't think he's a murderer. However, Johnson will sniff out his lying and have him locked up by sunset tomorrow. He's a good cop, but not a good investigator. You did not hear that from me." He steps away, and with a slow turn takes in everything around us. I do the same, and then the squawk of a microphone pulls our attention to the stage.

The band starts with shout-outs to the crowd and initial introductions; then the music starts with a popular country song about the beach. The crowd of about a hundred roars its approval as it sings along. Behind the band, clouds on the horizon wait for the sun to drop into them. The wide river that cuts off the island from the mainland is still, except for where a boat is leaving the marina and causing a wake. I spot Annie and Lucy in a crowd of people near the front of the stage. How much fun it would be to join them, but…

Officer Greyson watches over his town, thumbs hooked in his utility belt, and as I step out in front of him, I wave, then point down the side street. I've turned back the way I came. He follows my point, then nods, approving of my direction.

I'm going home.

When I left our house earlier, tennis shoes ready to walk off my anxiety, it was because Officer Greyson is right. Craig didn't want to discuss the murder or the marina or anything else because he had work to do. My default has always been that when Craig has work to do, that's what needs to be done. I didn't push back when he missed family events or when I thought he was too sick to work or when the kids needed help with homework.

I see now that he can ignore the world because I always kept the world at bay. Now it looks ridiculous. What did I think he was doing, curing cancer? Solving world hunger? How can two supposedly intelligent people let their lives get so out of balance?

The live music fades as I get closer to our street. There are a few people out walking their dogs, and the air is quite a bit cooler than it has been the last few nights. It feels like spring to me, but everyone today was complaining about winter coming back. Guess I still have my northern blood. The musical background is nice for my walk. When I look before crossing the street to get to our house, I see Craig walking away from me up the opposite street. So, I turn left and follow him. Maybe he's realizing how out of balance things are, too, and is out looking to join me at Florida Friday. I jog a bit to catch up as he's almost a block ahead.

We can go downtown, have a drink outside somewhere, and listen to the music, enjoy the sunset. That would be a much better setting for us to talk than in that dark house, which he said this morning is such a weight on him. Yes, my chest feels lighter just seeing him out like this. This is what we need, to get out of that house—together.

And yet... we're not together. Why am I indulging in all this fairytale hoping? At least I can find out where he's going unlike the last few times he's disappeared. So, at the next street, I wait as a car goes by. When the car pulls away, I see Craig turn onto a walkway behind a large bush. I cross the street and try to look past the flowering bushes to where he went. As I come to the opening he disappeared into, I see the sign for Bellington Manor Inn.

I peek around the tall bush and watch as the front door is thrown open. The man standing there is of an average height, with average hair and average clothes, yet as he speaks my mouth falls open and hangs there. "C. J., old friend, good to see you again," the man says, and I can hear others welcoming my husband, too. Then the door is closed and the porch is empty.

Now what?

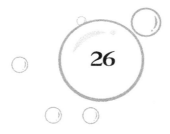

26

"What are you doing out here sneaking around?" a voice says. Its point is punctuated by a jab in my back.

Spinning around, I see the older woman who lives in the cottage on these grounds. "Charlotte! You scared me!"

She's wearing a long, beige sleeveless jacket over beige pants and a light-colored turtleneck and using a cane, one of those with four little legs at the bottom. The cane she used to poke me. With her shoulders squared, she's leaning on the cane, and she squints at me as she says, "I scared you because you were sneaking around." She pokes the cane at my legs. "Come on. Go on up the sidewalk. Into the house. No sneaking around here, go right up to the front door."

"Oh, but I can't. That was my husband."

That stops the poking. "That was C. J.? This damn twilight is murder on my eyes. I can't see a thing. Well, if it was your husband, that's more reason than ever to go on in, right?" She's not only squinting at me now; she's cocked her head like she knows something.

Maybe she's the one sneaking around. I squint right back at her and ask, "But what's Craig doing here? Was the man that opened the door your son?"

She grunts and leans on her cane with both hands. "Yes, of course. Frank Bellington the Third. He and that wife of his have cocktails about this time every night with their guests and invited friends. It just so happens to be the time I try to walk around the block each evening." Her lips turn up into a grin, or maybe a grimace. "I try to keep an eye on things." She mumbles, "Strangers drinking in my house," as she turns and starts walking away, back down the sidewalk toward the path Annie and I took to her cottage the other day.

"Can I walk with you?" I ask. "I don't think I should interrupt the party. I'll just wait to talk to Craig at home."

She doesn't slow down or answer, but she waves her arm for me to follow along. "You know Pierson's mother and wife are there right? Having drinks with your husband right now."

"I did hear they were staying there. I guess Mrs. Mantelle is friends with your son and daughter-in-law?"

As the sun dips below the horizon there's a noticeable darkening around me. As we turn the corner, Charlotte Bellington looks up at me. "And business partners, now that Pierson is gone. My greedy son Frank invested heavily in Pierson's plans."

"Leigh Anne, Pierson's mother, is involved in the marina business?"

Charlotte stops and looks through a little clearing at the big, lit-up manor house. "Leigh Anne? No, Saundra, Pierson's wife—the other Mrs. Mantelle, except that name's not good enough for her. Her father is Daniel York. *The* Daniel York."

We hear another welcome from Charlotte's son as someone else has joined the party. She cocks her head at me. This time she's definitely wearing a grin. "Want to have some fun?"

My tennis shoes come in handy as we turn off the path to her cottage and walk up the side of the back gardens. She has on sturdy old lady shoes, as she calls them, so we are both pretty quiet. Away from the lighted windows in the big house, off to the side, is a small, unadorned door. It's old and reminds me of a servant' entrance. Deep in the shadows of the old trees, away from the designed layout of landscape lights, I doubt we could be seen even by someone in the backyard. However, I feel better that it's empty, because now we are most definitely sneaking.

Charlotte grasps the handle of the door and twists it hard to the left, then pulls the door to her. The door eases open as she slowly pulls it. She turns to me and whispers, "They keep this door locked, but I lived in this house over sixty years before they threw me out. I know how to get past these old locks."

Up a handful of uneven concrete stairs, we enter a dark hallway, then follow voices and dim light to an open doorway. Charlotte peeks out, reporting back: "Coast is clear."

We scamper across the doorway that leads to the kitchen. Charlotte left her cane out in the bushes, said she didn't need it in the house. We are in another dark hallway, and I can see a laundry room through a half-closed door on the wall beside us. The wall to our right is solid and dark, but there is muted light up ahead, coming through narrow slots at about shoulder height. When we get to the slots, Charlotte turns around and holds her finger up in front of her mouth. At the lines of light she reaches up and releases a piece of wallpaper so that it falls down the wall a few inches.

She slides out a piece of thin cardboard, and light fills the area directly in front of us. She waves at me to stand next to her, so I do. We both look out through the inch-high slot.

It's a den, or maybe an old-fashioned library. There are walls of books, and I realize we are behind a bookcase ourselves. We are looking out above a row of books and below the next shelf. There's Craig and the man from the front door, Charlotte's son, Frank. Leigh Anne Mantelle is there, sitting on a love seat, holding a drink, with her legs crossed far too alluringly for a married woman of her age. However, that may just be my jealousy speaking because she looks really good. Her dark hair is down, and she's wearing a short, cream-colored dress that shows off her tan and her cleavage. Another woman comes into the room and sits beside her on the love seat. She's attractive, too, but doesn't look as athletic. She's about the same age as Leigh Anne, so I'm thinking she may be the lady of the house, Charlotte's daughter-in-law. We don't have a full view of the room, so I'm maneuvering around to see who's closest to the wall because those are the voices we can hear.

With a tinkling of ice in a glass, a woman to my right says in a low voice, "Everyone is running scared. Those cowards don't want to touch Sophia now, and the cowards here are denying everything."

Another woman responds. "Pierson sure didn't do any of us any favors getting himself killed like that. Can I top off your drink?" I'd thought the woman sitting beside Leigh Anne was Charlotte's daughter-in-law, but this woman sounds like the hostess, offering to refill a drink. I bend close to Charlotte's ear and ask as I point in the direction of the last voice, "Is that your daughter-in-law?"

Charlotte shakes her head and points to the woman sitting with Leigh Anne. I point again at the woman we can't see and mouth, "Who?"

She shrugs and shakes her head. As the first woman, the one who called someone cowards, walks into the center of the room, I'm shocked to see that I recognize her. It's Sheryl-Lee, the woman on the city council that I had lunch with. She walks up to Craig and puts her hand on his shoulder. I almost laugh when he jumps. He's not comfortable with strangers touching him. He steps away from her, then walks straight toward us. I back up and gasp, which gets me a sharp look from Charlotte. She slides the piece of cardboard back in place, tacks the wallpaper back up, and motions for me to leave. We sneak out the way we came in, and I hold her arm until we get to where she left her cane. She then scuttles away from me.

"Charlotte, I'm sorry. They didn't hear me."

I follow her toward her cottage, but she turns on me.

"No, they didn't hear you, but they could've." She stares at me for a moment, then shakes her head. "I'm processing why in the world I showed that to you. What was I thinking? I barely know you."

"Well, I appreciate it, I guess." I can't hold in a sigh. "What that woman said about Pierson's death was just awful. And seeing Sheryl-Lee touch my husband makes my skin crawl. You have no guess who the woman talking to Sheryl-Lee was? It couldn't have been Pierson's wife. Not with what she said about his death. Right? And who would Sheryl-Lee be calling cowards that backed out? The town? Or maybe the Yorks you mentioned?"

Charlotte shuffles on to her door. "I have no idea. I'm tired now. Do I need to tell you I don't want anyone else to know about this?"

"But I need to talk about it with Annie and Lucy. See what they think. Get them to help me figure out what's going on. What if the murderer was in that room?"

She opens her door, steps inside, then speaks to me past the half-closed door. "Tell them you were eavesdropping, maybe outside one of the windows, but keep my name out of it. You hear me? I don't need anyone knowing all my tricks with *my* house." She pulls her cane in, closes the door, and clicks it locked.

The path to her door is lit with a row of solar lights along the ground. They continue to the side of the property, so I follow them out of the dark, jungly area as the bugs and frogs really start chirping. I check before I step out onto the sidewalk that it's empty. I cross over the street there instead of walking back up to the corner. Trying to act like I'm just out for a walk, I swing my arms and hum to the Eagles song I can hear the band playing in the distance. At the corner I nonchalantly look at the entrance to Bellington Manor Inn, where Charlotte had scared me earlier.

I pause, stepping behind a large, moss-covered tree. There are people standing out on the sidewalk. I see Frank Bellington and Craig and the pale dress Leigh Anne was wearing. Is any shade of white appropriate when your son was just killed? Anyway, Craig steps away from the entrance, and hell's bells, look who's walking with him—Sheryl-Lee. I wait to let them turn the corner and get ahead of me. Then I follow on this side of the road, the side our house is on. Craig is walking fast, and when he gets to the gate, he darts ahead of her a bit. They talk for a minute, and then he sharply turns and strides up the long drive. I wait in the shadows while he walks into our house and she walks toward the marina and the music. Then, just as I get ready to step out, I see someone across the street trip on one of the roots that invade the sidewalks in this area. The shadows are deep there, and I can't see much except that the person gets up and darts around the far corner.

Someone was watching Craig and Sheryl-Lee.

Or were they watching me?

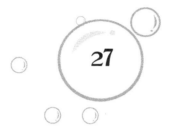

27

Dashing up to our gate, sliding through it, then running full tilt up the sidewalk, up the steps, across the porch, and finally into our house, I feel like I did when we were kids and would scare ourselves out in the backyard with ghost stories. That mad rush to get inside to light and safety.

Craig steps out of the kitchen. "Jewel? What are you doing? Where have you been? We were invited out for cocktails, and I couldn't find you. Why didn't you take your phone?"

"No pockets. I was just going out for a quick walk," I spit out while catching my breath against the front door. "Cocktails? Where?" This is a possibly pleasant surprise. I thought I'd have to drag all of this out of him.

"Bellington Manor Inn, that huge place just

up the street. Can you believe I know the owner?" He walks over to the sofa, but before he sits down, he turns to me. "Oh, I'm having some wine. Can I get you a glass?" He pauses and stares at me. "Are you okay?"

"Sure. I mean, sure, I'm okay." I walk toward the kitchen, turning on lamps as I go and trying to breathe normally. "You sit down, I'll get myself a glass." Opening the fridge I say loudly, "What's it like? The manor? What are the owners like?"

"Big. The house, not the owners. And that woman that came by the other day, Pierson's mother? She's staying there, so she was there along with Pierson's wife."

So that probably was his wife that was so awful about his death. I shiver, then decide to sit on the other end of the sofa. As I sit Craig reaches out his glass to clink with mine. "To Friday," he says with a smile.

After a sip, I nudge him on. "So who else was there?"

He shakes his head a bit, then rolls his eyes. "This councilwoman, King is her name, I think. She comes on pretty strong. Frank warned me about her."

"Warned you how?"

"You're going to laugh at this, but apparently

she's known for sleeping around with influential men. For some reason Frank thinks I'm influential." He chuckles as he looks at the wine in his glass.

"So, did she come on to you?"

He laughs and raises his eyebrows. "She did kind of. Followed me right to our gate. What is it with women like that?"

Poor Craig. He's never picked up on women flirting with him. He's never seen himself as attractive, and looking at him now I realize he's probably at this age the most attractive he's ever been. I really hadn't noticed that. With a laugh, hiding a bit of sadness, I say, "I don't know. I actually had lunch with her the other day. She's best friends with one of Annie's daughters."

I sit my glass down and turn toward him, tucking my leg up on the couch. "Listen, we need to talk. I ran into Officer Greyson downtown. He said he'd been here to talk to you?"

"Yeah, this afternoon, but I had a conference call so I rushed him along. I hate that they haven't solved this murder yet, but that's not my job. It's their job. And since apparently I won't be getting the marina position, I need to keep the job I have now."

"If you get arrested for murder, you won't be able to do either job, right?"

He scoffs, pulling his chin in. "How could I be arrested for murder? Don't exaggerate, Jewel. That's not like you." He stiffens and leans away from me.

"Greyson says the department's lead investigator is coming home early from vacation specifically to work this case. He says he likes to make arrests, and since you're the one obviously not being truthful, you'll be his first suspect."

I brace for Craig's affront at my accusation. Instead he sighs and hangs his head, his chin resting on his chest. Then he tips his head up and he wrinkles his nose at me. "I'm not a very good liar, am I?"

"No." I reach out a hand and lay it on his arm. "Talk to me. Let's figure this out. I promise I won't be mad."

He bites his lip and then shakes his head a few times, as though he's psyching himself up for our talk. "Okay, first the inheritance. Wait, I'm getting some more wine. Can I get you some?" he asks as he stands up.

"I'll join you. I'm actually starving. Did you eat something earlier?" I follow him into the kitchen.

"Just finished up that pasta you brought home last weekend from the Italian place. I could eat something." He pulls open the fridge and grabs the bottle of white wine. "Not much to eat in here."

"I wasn't counting on you being home all week."

I refill our glasses while he rummages in the drawers of the fridge. He pulls out some cheese. "Do we have bread? How's a grilled cheese sound?"

"Yes, we have some of that five-grain bread. Never made grilled cheeses with it, but it sounds delicious." I hand him his glass and reach around him to get the butter from the door before he closes the refrigerator.

We work together at the simple task of putting together grilled cheese sandwiches. As we do he fills me in on the inheritance and how the five-year agreement works. "I just had to agree to not sell the house for five years, but there was nothing in the contract about not trading it, so that's where the Pierson deal came in. I had the real estate lawyer look it all over, and while he said we might be able to get out of the inheritance rules, he didn't think any of it was too out of line."

I watch the butter begin to sizzle to avoid looking at my husband. "But why didn't you tell me?"

I can almost hear him shrug before he says,

"I didn't think you'd agree to it. No, that's not exactly right." He pauses long enough that I look away from the butter and at him. "Honestly, I don't think I thought you'd care. You seemed in such a hurry to move forward, do something, anything, and this was right there in front of us." He shakes his head as he looks at me. "We really didn't talk much at all about it, did we?"

"No, we didn't. Hand me the bread." I lay down two slices in the browning butter, add slices of cheese, then add the last two pieces of bread.

He picks up his glass of wine, hands me mine, then leans against the counter. "Anyway. Pierson contacted me almost immediately via email once I signed the inheritance papers. Maybe he didn't know about it until it was filed or something, I don't know. At first he told me how we'd have to get together and catch up. And you know that's just not me, so I shut that down pretty quick. But he had all these questions about our plans, my career, the house, so I answered those but tried to make it clear I wasn't interested in getting to know each other. He was so much younger than us, so I just didn't see the purpose. Then when we got here and I saw this place—not just this house, but the town—it all came back. This whole small-town thing where your name is everything. Well, you might've noticed, I couldn't get out of here fast enough. Another confession. The company didn't call begging me to take this job in South Florida. I called them begging. Cut my rate and everything."

I flip the sandwiches and press down hard on each of them with the spatula. Maybe a little too hard. I knew it. I knew he wanted to go back to work all along and just refused to acknowledge it. Taking a deep breath, I tell my husband his big secret wasn't such a big secret. "I guess I knew all along you weren't ready to retire. You love your job. It's who you are."

"Sorry, Jewel, but..." He shrugs, then gets two plates out of the cabinet. "Anyway, when Pierson told me his real reason for reaching out, well, I thought maybe if we could unload this house, live down at the marina for a year or two, it'd really be a whole new start for us."

"So why couldn't you tell me about that?"

"Pierson told me you couldn't know. No one could know. By that time I was in South Florida and was really just letting him and the York people handle it." As I hand him his plate, he meets my eyes. "Plus, you know how I am when I'm on a job."

"Yes. I know." I sit across from him at the table. "So, the York people? Who are they?"

"That's the company Pierson works for. His wife's family. Matter of fact she's the CEO. Big company, mostly in real estate, I believe. Big players down south." As he talks I remember how Charlotte sounded when she mentioned Pierson's wife's father, Daniel York.

As we eat, I immediately feel better, and my mind seems to wake up. "Your laptop? Was that what someone broke in for?"

He grins. "It was. How did you know that?"

"Cherry saw the cords and realized something was missing. So who took it?"

"Don't know. I just know Ray Barnette, that councilman that owns all the trash stuff? He called and said he had it. Honestly, I hadn't missed it until he called. Didn't want to call the police up and admit I hadn't missed it. I figured they had enough to deal with with the murder."

As his voice trails off like he's explained it all, I prod him. "So? What else did he say when he told you he had it?"

He pops the last bite of grilled cheese in his mouth and while he chews he frowns like what Ray had to say is not worth remembering. "Just that the person that took it was really sorry and that it was a mistake. Since I was out of the running for the marina job, I didn't care who knew what the plans were. The rest of the stuff on the laptop was personal stuff, correspondence and such. Barnette said it was a mistake. I was just glad to get it back. I hated the idea of filling out an insurance claim for it."

The thing about Craig not being able to lie is that he's also not able to decipher when someone else is lying. He just doesn't think people have ulterior motives. He accepts everything at face value like lines on his engineering sketches. They are what they are.

"You have to tell the police this," I say. "It may have something to do with the murder."

"My personal laptop? I don't see how." He stands up. "But if you think it'll help, sure. I'll tell this detective tomorrow. All I know is I have to be back on the jobsite Monday morning, so they need to get things figured out." He picks up both our plates, crosses the kitchen with them, and slides them into the dishwasher.

I turn around in my chair to see him. "So since we've been here, have you met Pierson's wife? What's her name, Sandra? No, Saundra."

"Nope, didn't meet her until tonight, but I was supposed to meet with her a couple times before. Twice Pierson set up appointments for me with her that were cancelled after I got there.

The other night, I drove all the way down to Jacksonville to meet her, but she never showed. Later Pierson called to say she'd had something come up, like I hadn't just driven an hour out of my way."

"So that's where you were. Why didn't you tell me?"

He shrugs. "I told you, he said no one could know. Not even you."

That's Craig. Ever the rule-follower. "So, when was the other time you were supposed to meet her?"

"The day I was at the marina. She was supposed to meet me on the boat, but when I got almost to the boat, Pierson met me on the dock and said she wasn't even in town. He acted like he was in a hurry to get rid of me, and he was really mad when I told him I had to talk to his wife. He said that he was handling everything and that his wife wasn't involved in our deal." He's wiping down the counters as he continues. "That made me mad because he's always acted like it was a big project for York and that really impressed me. He had said they wanted to give me a huge raise and all, but then the CEO, Saundra York, doesn't even know about the deal?"

My eyes are bugging out of my head. "Did you tell the police all this?"

"Of course not!" He turns to me with his hands on his hips like he's explaining all of this to a child. "Remember, I told them I wasn't at the marina. Besides, Pierson and I just talked for a few minutes and we weren't on the boat. It wasn't a meeting like everyone, including you, keeps asking about. By the time I left the dock, I was frustrated, felt like a dupe. So I left there that day determined it was all over. I decided to ignore that it ever happened. Plus, you seemed happy enough here, and I had the job in South Florida that could easily last close to five years. I decided I could manage to live here a weekend or so a month." He smiles and takes a deep breath. "Living in a holding pattern isn't ideal, but we've made it work okay, right?"

I stand up, trying to breathe regularly. "Craig. Forget the marriage. We'll deal with that later, but this, all this you just told me is what the police need to know. This is why you're under suspicion—the police know there's more to this story. Did you ever think Saundra could've been setting you up for her husband's murder? She sent you onto the boat when he's with his little girlfriend? Was there ever really even a deal like the one he was selling you? If she's the CEO and her father is the owner, they had to know what he was doing." I walk away from my husband in disbelief that he can be this obtuse. This arrogant.

He follows me. "His girlfriend? I thought that was his daughter! She was younger than our girls."

"Exactly. These are not nice, normal people!"

My phone buzzes from the coffee table in the living room. I pick it up to read the text and say, "Annie wants to talk."

I text her back, "In a minute." The text gives me a moment to breathe and calm down. Out of the corner of my eye I watch as Craig sits on the chair beside the staircase.

He waits until I turn fully around. "I see what you're saying. I just couldn't imagine any of this had anything to do with Pierson being killed. I didn't really think I was lying because I don't have anything to lie to the police about. And I should've obviously told you about the marina plan, but I just didn't see the need to get you upset if it never turned out. But I should've trusted you. Sorry about that. About it all."

"Okay. But you have told me everything now, right?"

"Right." He stands up, and with his hands

on his hips, he looks around. "Looks like we're stuck with this old place for a while."

"Pierson really wanted the house?" I raise my eyebrows as I look around. "Seems kind of odd since he's apparently never lived on Sophia Island. He grew up and lives down in some fancy place called Ponte Vedra."

"Maybe he only wanted to live here if he got the family mansion. I got the feeling it was more for his wife. He said she'd always loved it. Wanted to fix it up to its original glory." He looks up the stairs. "While you call Annie, I'm going up to take a shower and then read some stuff for work, but now that you've got me thinking, I'm wondering if I should call Officer Greyson and tell him I'd like to meet with him first thing in the morning to lay it all out for him."

My shoulders relax for the first time in days, and the wrinkles in my forehead release. "Yes. I think that's a wonderful idea. I can sit in with you if you'd like. He can come here."

He studies me for a moment. "Do you think you can be happy here? Hold things together for a few years?"

I smile at him but shake my head a bit. "Let's just get this murder thing off our plate. Then we can think about being happy, okay?"

"Okay." As he jogs up the stairs he says, "I'm

glad all this will be over tomorrow. Then you won't have to mess around with Annie and all those ladies always barging in here." He turns and gives me a nod. "Just the way you like things, nice and quiet."

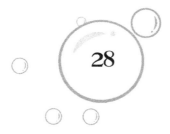

28

Text messages back and forth finally convince me to join Annie and Lucy where they are having a drink only two blocks from our house. It seems like it's at least midnight with all that's happened, but Annie pointed out it is only nine o'clock. After a quick change upstairs and an even quicker chat with Craig, I head out the door.

On the front porch with the big door shut behind me, I can admit that I'd gone upstairs not planning on changing, not planning on going out. Craig was coming out of the shower. We'd both had a glass or two of wine. We'd actually talked for the first time in a long time. Besides, it is Friday night.

But—well, there was nothing there. So much nothing it was almost embarrassing. I don't understand, and the only comfort I can find is that he can't seem to understand either. It was downright awkward. Tears spring to my eyes, and I wipe them away, then jog down the wide porch steps. I'd thrown on a long, navy-blue jersey dress with long sleeves and a scoop neckline while Craig had retreated back into the bathroom behind another closed door.

My flat sandals slap the sidewalk, and as I pass through the gate, I remember how frightened I was when I came home only an hour ago.

That makes me pause, but the moon is out in a sultry, midnight-blue sky. Distant laughter is accented by the frogs and bugs, and something is blooming that smells like cotton candy. There's a warmth in the humid air that reminds me of all those sayings and songs about Southern nights. No reason to be scared, right?

Besides, going back inside that house is not an option.

I'm glad to be meeting my friends at Pavers as I've not been there yet. It's off Centre Street, and while there is some indoor seating, mostly it's known for its garden area. Pavers are those stones used in gardens and patios, and at the restaurant, mostly known for their crepes, they form a wide open patio interspersed with chairs, fire pits, and small gardens. I don't know why we haven't tried it except that there are so many restaurants here and so little time.

Lights in the trees, music, and the smell of food draw me in.

"Girl! You did come!" Annie shouts. She holds a hand out and up to me. "I'd get up and hug you, but this couch is just too low. Sit right there!"

Annie's natural exuberance has been lubricated by alcohol. She's all smiles and bright eyes, along with being louder than usual. But she's so charming, who cares? Annie has on leggings and a long, flowy, olive-colored shirt with tight arms and a low-cut front. She's wearing a thick gold necklace with her usual collection of bracelets, and in the light from the fire pit in front of her, she looks like a queen. Sitting beside her is Ray Barnette. He has his arm tucked inside her elbow. On the side Annie directed me to, Lucy and another lady I don't know are seated on two wide, cushioned chairs.

Lucy jumps up from her seat to hug me. "Oh, Jewel, you just missed meeting Davis! He drove in from Atlanta today and was too exhausted to stay. But this is Aunt Jean. She's been wanting to meet you!" Lucy and Jean resemble each other in that they are both petite and blonde. Lucy looks more like her aunt than her mother, Birdie, but they all look like family. Jean is obviously Birdie's much younger sister.

"So you're Jewel Mantelle, new owner of the Mantelle Mansion," Jean says as she looks me up and down. She pats the cushion of Lucy's chair. "Come sit here. Lucy can move down now that Davis finally left and there's no need to keep him behind her protective wall."

"Aunt Jean, be nice," Lucy says with a swat at her aunt's knee. However, she does move down to the chair I'm standing next to, which makes a place for me between her and her aunt.

Annie practically heehaws as she wags a finger at Jean. "Your jealousy is showing, Jean. You know you're too old for Davis."

"Pshaw, I'm only ten or so years older than my dear niece here. And for a piece of Davis Reynolds, I'd lie about my age."

"Like you don't lie about your age already," Lucy says with an eye roll. "Ignore her, Jewel. Why didn't you come to Florida Friday? We had you a seat and everything."

"That seems like a million years ago," I say. "I did come downtown, but then I ran into Officer Greyson—oh, yes." As a waitress appears asking if I'd like a drink, I stop and look around. "Wine, I guess. White, pinot grigio?" She walks off, and I proceed to tell them all about what

Greyson said. They frown and nod at the mention of Detective Johnson. I skip the part about Charlotte's Peeping-Tom hallway at Bellington Manor Inn and move on to my conversation with Craig. I of course neglect to share the more intimate, and disappointing, parts.

"Where is Craig?" Ray asks. "Why didn't he come with you?"

"He had some work to catch up on," I say with a tight smile. Everyone catches the awkwardness, and Lucy pats my knee.

Ray takes his arm from around Annie and leans forward. "You said he came clean, so I'm hoping he told you about the laptop."

"Yes, but who took it in the first place?" I ask.

"Exactly! Ray won't tell us!" Annie exclaims. "Says it's personal and he promised not to tell."

Lucy shushes Annie, then turns to me. "He says it has nothing to do with the murder and that it was all a mistake."

"Just doing a favor for an old friend," he says as he leans back and nods at the waitress bringing my drink. When she leaves, he speaks in a low voice. "Believe you me, this marina debacle is what caused Pierson Mantelle to lose his life."

Sitting my glass of wine on the table in front

of me, I return his focus. "So, Mr. Barnette, are you still up for the marina job?"

"Naw, whole thing can't happen now. Not with everyone knowing everything. This kind of plan has to be kept quiet until things are figured out so the facts don't get thrown out of proportion and such. You know how folks get. Plus, I'm not sure we could've controlled York like we wanted to. I've done some more studying on the marinas they've bought down south, and in a year or two the towns seem to lose all control. Part of my thinking was that I could control the growth, only do what was good for Sophia. I may sound and act like a good ol' boy from the country, but I'm a lot smarter than I look." He winks and reaches his arm around Annie to squeeze her. "I keep trying to convince this girl here she could do worse."

Annie giggles, and Jean mutters, "Oh my lord," under her breath.

"So who do you think benefitted the most from Pierson's death? Or do you think it was someone acting in anger over the deal falling apart?" I ask so only our little group can hear.

Jean clears her throat. "Well, look who just showed up." Lucy's aunt has lifted her head high, and in the firelight I can see her full head of hair is more gray than blonde.

At a low table like ours, closer to the restaurant's guitar player, a seated group is welcoming more guests who just arrived. The guests are the very people I'd watched earlier through a hidden spy hole in an old house. Heat floods my face even though no one here knows. I recognize Frank Bellingham, his wife, and Leigh Anne Mantelle in her short, white dress. The other woman with them has luxurious auburn hair, which catches flashes of the fire. Her black dress is conservative, in a wrap style that emphasizes her shape. She's wearing very nice black high heels. Pumps with a red sole, I notice, as she takes a seat.

"Who's that? The one in the black dress."

"Saundra York, Pierson's wife," Ray says. "Guess her last name is Mantelle, but from what I know she never used it. I mean, if you're a York, why not stay a York?" He looks at me. "No offense, Mrs. Mantelle."

"None taken. She sure is beautiful."

Annie exclaims, "Don't that beat all!" She quickly looks from us and lowers her voice. "Don't that beat all to have a wife what looks like that and you gotta have floozies on the side? I will never understand that. Never!"

Jean smirks. "Doesn't look to me like she'd be

all that fun in the dark. I mean, once you turn off the lights, looks don't matter."

Lucy rolls her eyes at her aunt as she stands up. "I haven't offered my condolences, so I'm going to go do it right now, see if I can pick up any vibes from the widow and the bereaved mother. Law, that dress of Leigh Anne's is clear up to her, well, you know what. Anyone else want to come?"

Annie and Ray shake their heads and take another sip of their drinks. Jean considers, then says, "No, I'm mighty comfortable here. Besides, I need to talk to Jewel."

Lucy makes her way across the patio. She's wearing high wedge sandals and a long, striped wrap shirt over dark leggings. She makes her way across, stopping to speak with virtually every table. "That niece of mine is a born politician," Jean says. "So, Jewel, your house. Tell me about it. What do you plan to do with it? What kind of shape is it in? Can I come see it? Is it haunted?" She ends her barrage of questions with an intense stare.

"Well, I don't think it's haunted, but then I don't have a good feel for that kind of thing. It's creaky and kind of noisy sometimes, but I assume that's how all old houses are. As for plans, we don't have any. It's not in awful shape, but it sure is full of stuff. We don't know enough to know if it's good stuff or not. And, of course, you're more than welcome to come see it. Hopefully Craig will get this whole murder thing behind us when he talks to Officer Greyson tomorrow."

Annie holds up her glass. "Let's toast to that. However, we're not really any closer to finding out who murdered Pierson. So much for being detectives. Of course, Aiden says the police aren't any further ahead either. That's why Detective Johnson is coming back from vacation early."

I shift my focus to Annie's beau. "Ray, when you were on the boat with Pierson, what happened? Did he say anything?"

Ray shrugs. "Like I told the police, he was real disgruntled. Agitated. Didn't say why exactly, except he couldn't wait to get done here."

"Here?" I ask. "You mean his business that day?"

The big man shakes his head and rubs his beard with the hand not wrapped around Annie. "No, he actually said he hated Sophia and that he wanted this whole thing to be over. He planned on never sailing his boat back to this island for the rest of his life. That turned me off real bad, as I think this is God's favorite place on earth."

This shocks me. "What? But his wife wanted our house! That was the whole deal with Craig giving him the house for the condo and the job at the marina."

Ray tips up his glass to dislodge ice into his open mouth. As he crunches it he says, "If that's all true, I guess I was never really in the running for the job. Maybe as a backup, or to grease the wheels since I am on the commission. That jackass sure played me." He huffs and shakes his head. "Pardon the language, ladies." Annie pats his knee.

Jean flicks her hand at me. She taps my arm and with a shift of her eyes directs my attention across the patio to where Lucy stands next to Saundra York. That red-soled designer shoe shines like a beacon along with her big watch and jeweled fingers. Jean's graveled voice matches her cynically arched eyebrow. "Really? *She* wants to live in *your* house?"

"Well, that's what Craig said Pierson told him." With us still staring, Lucy turns and heads back to us.

"I'm ready to go," she says when she reaches our table. "Aunt Jean, you ready?"

"Sure, but how are things over there?"

Lucy sniffs, not in sadness I realize, but in anger. She shifts her hips and tips her head down to us. "It's cold over there. Very cold. Asking about funeral details was as worthwhile as if I'd asked when the next high tide is. Scratch that, that's general knowledge for folks here. I never met Pierson Mantelle, but I can't help but feel sorry for him with two such, uh, well, *women* in his life. Let's go." She flips around and starts across the patio. This time she doesn't acknowledge anyone; she's just hell-bent on getting to her destination. Jean frowns at all of us, tells me she'll talk to me soon, and then she hurries off after her niece.

"Guess it's time for me to go home, too," Ray says as he pushes himself up to the edge of the couch. "Sure will be a long drive. Wish I had a place to stay right here on the island." He waggles his eyebrows at Annie.

She slaps his leg. "And a frog wishes it had wings so it wouldn't bump its behind on the ground when it hops. Help me up out of this thing."

When we are all standing, I look around at the table. "I never paid my bill. Do we pay on the way out?"

Ray winks at me. "I got it. Told the waitress to put it on my tab. I'll settle up on the way out." He waves away my thanks, then tries one more pass at Annie, which she rebuffs.

She pushes his chest, but her hand lingers for a minute. "You go home. My car is toward Jewel's house, so we're going to go out this way and walk together." He leans forward for a kiss, but she ignores him and points me toward a back gate.

We step between the small bushes onto the sidewalk, and I nudge her. "He seems awful sweet on you."

"Yeah, and I like him, but, well, I've just never seen a man that don't want to be king when he finally gets a queen. And I'm too old to deal with a king. But I don't want to talk about all that." We walk side by side away from Pavers, and as the sounds drop off, we turn into a small parking lot on our left. We step into deeper shadows, but with a push of a button, the interior of Annie's car lights up. "Get in and I'll give you a ride home."

"I'm okay. It's only a couple blocks. Not even a couple from here. I'm in no hurry."

Annie leans against the car. "You seem sad, honey. What's going on?"

I join her, leaning on her car with a sigh. "Nothing really. Craig and I are just not connecting. At least when he's on the road I can pretend we do." I try to laugh, but it comes out more like another sigh.

Annie give me a lopsided smile. "Being married is tough. My husband and I were good together, but we always had the kids around so I don't know how we'd have done without buffers or distractions. Not sure what it would've been like being together twenty-four seven." She inhales. "That's a lot of together."

"Talk about marriage being tough, what about Pierson and his wife?" I try to think of a way to mention what I heard through the bookcase at Bellington Manor. "Pierson's wife sure doesn't seem to be very broken up about her husband's death. You know, I overheard her being quite flippant about it. Something like him getting himself killed caused a lot of problems."

Annie swings her head toward me. "Overheard? Where would you overhear something like that?"

I only shrug, and Annie squints her eyes at me. "Aiden hasn't mentioned them talking to the wife, but surely they did, right? It sounds like her family has a lot of clout, though. Maybe they were able to put off the police just like the girlfriend's family." She shakes her head. "Wonder what that group said to set Lucy off like that. She was downright mad. The whole thing doesn't make a lot of sense."

For a moment we look up through the

long, graceful tree limbs draped in moss. Then I go back to our earlier conversation. "So Ray wouldn't say who took the laptop? That's just odd, isn't it? Someone broke into our home and no one thinks anything of it? And, wait." I turn to face her. "It was someone who knew about the window not locking. Who would know that?"

"Oh yeah. I'd forgotten that," she says. The light inside her car has gone out again, but our eyes have adjusted to the dim corner lot. The moon is still low in the sky, providing soft light. Annie crosses her arms, and her voice takes on a more determined tone. "One thing I know for sure is that I'm going to have to get better at taking notes to be a detective. There are too many things to remember and, don't tell anyone, but my memory isn't what it used to be." She ends with a nudge of her elbow at me.

On the sidewalk, we hear footsteps and look up to see Frank Bellington striding along in a hurry. Behind him, in no hurry but looking over her shoulder, comes his wife. Several paces behind her are Leigh Anne and her daughter-in-law, Saundra. Frank's light green shirt stands out in the gloom, as does his wife's light skirt and Leigh Anne's dress. Frank turns the corner, obviously headed home. When his wife arrives at the corner she calls for him to slow down, but he ignores her. She beckons for the women behind her to hurry up. They don't. She says something to them about having a drink before bed, then dashes ahead to catch up with her husband. Leigh Anne and Saundra make their way around the corner and head back to the manor house as well, though they take their own sweet time.

Annie and I don't speak until they are well out of sight, but then I stand up straight and step away from the car. "Have a good night, Annie. We'll let you know how things go with Officer Greyson in the morning." I am already halfway across the parking lot by the time Annie has once again clicked her key and lit her corner of the parking lot.

If that crew in front of me is going to have a nightcap, I think I should be there to hear it.

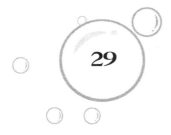

29

Sticking to the shadows, I follow the four toward Bellington Manor House. I cross the street before we get to the front entrance so that I am nowhere near the lamp post beside the sign for the inn. Their shoes on the wooden front steps seem loud in the stillness, but then again, I am listening extra hard. My flat sandals don't make a sound as I scurry across the intersection and paste myself against the tall bushes where Charlotte and I walked earlier. I never imagined just how good a choice my navy dress would be for night prowling. I dart inside the garden with just a glance to my right to make sure the lights in Charlotte's cottage are out.

The bugs and frogs in the garden stop talking with my incursion into their domain. I remember it happening earlier, too, so it doesn't freak me out that much. Even so, the property seems way, way too quiet. I finally let out my breath when I reach the side door and clasp my hand around the old metal knob. Just the few weeks in our old, cantankerous house have taught me a fine appreciation for knowing hardware tricks.

"And so," I mutter under my breath as I attempt to open the door, "Charlotte pulled up and then twisted hard to the left to get around this lock." But my hand still clasps a locked door. I try again. And again. Little variations on my pull and twist match small prayers for the nightcaps to extend into more than one. I'm sweating, and the perspiration makes it harder to twist the knob.

Wiping my hand on my dress, I take a deep breath and blow it out with the words, "One more time." This time, with me doing the exact same thing as the last dozen tries, the door swings open. I bustle in and close the door behind me. Down the little dark hall I hurry, remembering to check the kitchen before I cross the doorway. This time the kitchen lights are also out, so the laundry hallway before me is even darker. I've been here before, so it's not as scary.

Working so hard on the door makes me feel triumphant, so it's not until I reach to lower the piece of wallpaper that I really think about what

I'm doing—sneaking, or some might say breaking and entering—into a stranger's house. But then I hear voices and, well, I *am* already here...

Leigh Anne is sitting on the same couch as she was earlier, but this time she's alone. On the opposite side of the room, in my full view, Saundra has kicked off her designer pumps and has her feet propped up on the ottoman in front of her chair. She holds a drink in her hand. I can't see if the owners of the inn are in the room, but I get the feeling they are not.

"I've already made the arrangements for here. Funeral and burial on Sophia Island," Leigh Anne says. She also has a drink, but she's hunched over, forearms resting on her knees. I can feel, and see, the tension in her shoulders.

Her daughter-in-law laughs. "If so, you sure weren't forthcoming with that little lady from city hall that came to express her condolences."

"Why did you have to be so rude? Lucy Fellows is important here." Leigh Anne swallows and stretches her neck out. "We're friends."

My eyes widen. Apparently Saundra York also finds it hard to believe. "Really? Friends? Then why didn't you give her the funeral details?"

"You know I need, well, I need you to give me the—"

"Permission. Go ahead and say it. Go ahead and ask." The younger woman puts her feet on the floor and stands. "Go ahead and ask me for permission, but I've already told you the answer. You can make all the plans in the world, but they're not happening."

She carries her empty glass toward the bookshelf, and me. This makes my heart stop, but then I remember the bar is in this direction.

"My husband's funeral will be where we—and you, I might add—live," Saundra says. "Ponte Vedra. My only interest in this town is now dead. Literally."

I can no longer see Saundra, but I can hear her fixing her drink to my right. It's unnerving as Leigh Anne is staring at Saundra and consequently looking in my direction.

Saundra continues. "I am leaving this hole-in-the-wall town tomorrow with my husband's body and will never step foot here again, just as I told your friend. Lucy, did you say her name was?"

She steps out into the middle of the room. With her free hand, she picks up her red-soled shoes. As she straightens she says to her mother-in-law, "I'm taking my drink upstairs and going to bed. These old houses are depressing. I can see why *you* love them." As she gets to the hallway, with the stairs in the background, she turns to face Leigh Anne. "I'm just glad I discovered what your worthless son was up to before he could pull the trigger. We Yorks would never be interested in such a rundown marina as the one here. I'm actually kind of glad someone killed him before Daddy found out about his plan. It saved me a lot of embarrassment. Good night. See you at the funeral."

I step away from the hole in the wall and quickly slide the cardboard and wallpaper back in place. I don't want to watch Leigh Anne anymore. She's not my favorite person, but she doesn't deserve all that. It almost makes me wish Saundra was the murderer. If she talked that way about Sophia Island to Lucy, no wonder Lucy was so mad. Wait, I think. Maybe she is the murderer. Just how good is her alibi for last Wednesday?

I wait for a while and listen, but I don't hear any noise to tell me if Leigh Anne is still on the couch. If it were me, I wouldn't be able to stand, much less move. Lose your son and be left with Saundra York for your family? Poor thing. Creeping down the hall, I stop to listen again for a minute or two. Nothing. At the kitchen door, it looks as though nothing has changed. Still dark and empty. I cross the doorway, dart to the door, grasp the knob, and yank it open. The darkness is getting to me.

The night air welcomes me, and I take a deep breath as I step into the garden. Then my arm is grabbed and jerked to the side.

"Caught you," a voice growls. Then it climbs an octave as it yelps. "You're not Charlotte!"

The hand pulls me into the dim light, and I'm standing face to face with Leigh Anne Mantelle.

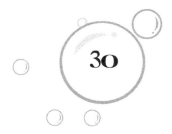

30

"What are you doing here?" Leigh Anne hisses in my face. She still has a tight grasp on my arm, but she backs off a few inches. She looks around us, then pushes me against the wall and leans against me hard.

"Oh, hi, Leigh Anne. What are you doing? I was looking for Charlotte. Did you see her?" I try to relax and calm my heart, but that's hard when I can see in Leigh Anne's eyes that she's putting two and two together.

"So Charlotte showed you her little spy hole. I forgot about it until I noticed something sparkling in the bookcase wall tonight. Must've been the light hitting that necklace."

My hand flies up to my throat, to the diamond necklace Craig gave me for our twenty-fifth anniversary. My sudden action causes her to press harder against me and to raise her other hand. A hand holding a big kitchen knife.

"Stand still!" she demands. The knife ensures I'll do exactly as she says.

"Okay, I'm not moving. You can put the knife down."

Leigh Anne licks her thin lips as she thinks. "Grabbed it to give that busybody Charlotte a real scare. I mean, I can scare her into keeping quiet, but you, you'll tell."

"Honestly, I don't know anything to tell," I protest. "Except that your daughter-in-law was really nasty to you." I try to inch my feet under my body so that I have some leverage to possibly push her away and run. I'm off balance with my shoulders and back smashed against the wall and my backside and legs at an awkward angle. She has one leg braced against the side of mine, which stops my legs from straightening. Her hand still holds my upper arm, and she's keeping me pinned on the wall with that tennis-playing arm. A very strong arm.

An arm strong enough to hurl a heavy pitcher of margaritas.

It's then that everything clicks for me.

She's the one who wants to live on Sophia Island.

She's the one who wants my house.

Suddenly a picture comes to mind of her opening our front door like she'd done it a million times before. And of course, she knew about the nonexistent lock on the back window.

Her face is only a few inches from mine. I chance a look to see if she realizes I've put it together, but she's busy with her own thoughts. She readjusts to pin me even closer to the wall, causing one of my sandals to slip. Now I'm even more at her mercy with only one leg for support.

"Leigh Anne, I'm falling. Let me stand up and we can talk."

She looks at me and sneers. "Talk? What do we have to talk about? You have my house. Pierson was supposed to get it for me, but then he got cold feet when that wife of his found out. I was so very mad at him. I didn't mean for him to die, I was just so mad. I mean, I waited so many years for Cora to finally die. And then she gives the house to C. J.? Not Edison and me?" Her eyes narrow. "Did your husband visit her? Did he help her take care of the house? Did you even know her?" She stops her rant to repeat herself. "Did you? Did you ever even meet that awful woman?"

She waits for an answer.

"Well, no," I say, "but honestly, you can have the house. We don't really want to live there.

My husband was willing to trade with Pierson. Here, let me up. This really hurts."

"Stay there. Let me think. If you're gone, your husband gone, then it'll go to Edison. He's basically a vegetable and stuck in that old folks' home, but he's still alive."

"Yes, we'll leave. Our family is all up north anyway. We'll leave tomorrow and it's all yours."

She laughs and lifts the knife again. "No, that won't work. Here you are, alone in a dark garden, and as for your husband, well, I know that house better than you could ever know it. Getting in and out of it is not a problem. Should've suffocated you with a pillow before now. Maybe poison for him? Or maybe he'll slit his wrists in despair at his wife's murder." She giggles. "They'll probably blame that crazy old woman Charlotte for this."

A phone ringing from the sidewalk on the other side of the bushes causes us both to look that direction. In that moment a dark body hurls into Leigh Anne and leaves her sprawled out on her back. I right myself against the wall, and I hear Annie shout, "Stay right there, Leigh Anne! The police just pulled up!"

Leigh Anne's white dress is shoved up, show-ing everything God gave her, but the best thing her dress does is give the police something to focus on as they come spilling into the garden with shouts and flashlights.

I can't see anything but a little circle of Annie's face. As she comes to hug me, in the light from all the flashlights, I see why. She's got a child's hoodie over her hair and bunched up under her chin.

"Oh, Annie. Thank God you came." In my relief, I can't help but start to laugh at the little circle of her face I can see. She moves back a step and tries to work the hoodie off her head.

"It's my grandson's and was the only dark thing I had in my car to cover my hair! Are you all right?"

Aiden catches up to us and grabs her. "Momma! Are you okay? I told you to wait for us to get here!"

She sways as she reaches out to her son. "I tried, but I, well, oh, I don't feel so good. Let's sit down." Aiden walks both of us to a garden bench. As all the back lights come on we hear voices from both the manor house and Charlotte's cottage. Leigh Anne is still on the ground. She's yelling something about being where she belongs and that I shouldn't be here.

Officer Greyson looks around and says soothingly, "Yes, ma'am. You're saying you're staying here, but Mrs. Mantelle, the other Mrs. Mantelle, is not staying here. We under—"

She stops him with a screech. "On Sophia Island, you idiot! I belong here, she doesn't. That house is mine, and I'll kill every last one of you if you get in my way! You think I won't? I killed my own son, why would you matter one little ant's hill to me? Let me up. I want to go home. My house is waiting on me!"

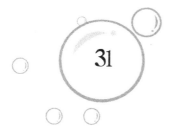

31

"See, if your arms weren't so skinny, she couldn't have held you against the wall like that," Annie says with another side hug for me. When she left the Bellingtons' last night she told me she'd be at our house at eight thirty sharp with food and the rest of the ladies to get the full story.

We'd all talked to the police for what seemed like hours. They'd brought Craig there, and by the time we got to leave our shock had worn off. We could barely crawl up the stairs to bed. However, it wasn't that easy for me to actually turn off my mind and go to sleep. The sun was fully up by the time I woke and found Craig was already up. Since it was already eight o'clock, I showered and dressed. I chose a long-sleeve cotton T-shirt, and as I pulled the sleeves down over my sore, bruised arms, tears threatened.

I've never been hurt intentionally. With a pair of shorts and my flip-flops, I headed down to see what the day had in store, but I already knew it wouldn't compare to yesterday. Thank goodness.

Downstairs Craig had the front door open, and I found that he'd moved some of our extra furniture onto the front porch. "It's too pretty to sit inside, but we don't have any outdoor furniture. Might as well use some of this overflow," he explained.

"Looks like some rundown shack with an old couch on the front porch," I told him as I hugged him. We heard car doors and pulled apart to begin taking coffee orders from Lucy, Tamela, Cherry, Annie, Aiden, and Officer Greyson.

Now, settled around the small side tables that hold our coffee cups and bags of fresh-baked treats from the farmers market, Annie and I share our stories. Again.

Officer Greyson reaches for another spanakopita. He's wearing casual clothes and is off duty, as is Aiden. They worked late into the night but said they'd see us early as planned, though it wouldn't be an official interview.

I return Annie's side hug. "You exploding into the garden was amazing. Good thought on covering that shining head of hair you've got. It was like a shadow bowling her over. And your phone ringing? How did you manage that at just the right moment?"

She shrugs. "I didn't. I'd taken it out and left it beside the sidewalk so it wouldn't make some silly noise and give me a way. I'd been texting with Aiden, and then I put on that little hoodie and was sneaking closer just to hear what she was saying. I'd seen she had that big ol' knife, but I didn't see any reason to really be afraid. Then I think I started putting things together about the same time as you did. The phone ringing was Amber calling to ask me about babysitting today! Liked to scared me to death, too. I think that's what made me jump her!"

Cherry pulls off the lightweight cardigan she's wearing over her dark red scrubs. She came here directly from her overnight shift at the hospital and looks wan in the morning light. "Maybe I'm just tired, but tell me again about this hole in the wall at the Bellingtons'. Annie, you knew about it?"

"I did, but I'd forgotten about it. When I was in elementary school I hung out with Charlotte's younger sister some. We'd spy on Charlotte when she'd have a date in there or when her parents had parties. It was just a little open space, more a crack between paneling pieces. Then that was wallpapered over, and well, we all grew up. But Charlotte said something a while ago that made me think she was spying on her son and daughter-in-law. When Jewel told me she'd 'overheard' Saundra saying such awful things about her husband, well, I guess it fell into place."

She rolls her eyes at us. "The way this one," she nudges me, "suddenly was in a hurry to go home right after Leigh Anne and them passed by tipped me off. I figured it couldn't hurt to check things out."

Aiden looks at his superior officer, and when he receives a nod, he looks at us and says, "That other Mrs. Mantelle really wanted this house. Apparently she was comfortable coming and going here while Miss Cora was in the loony bin."

Greyson stops him with a stern "Officer Bryan."

"Right, the, uh, the institution. Anyway, she just assumed her husband, Edison, would inherit it, so while she couldn't live outright in the house, apparently she'd just hang out here. Probably why so many people thought it was haunted through the years."

I shiver and pull my sleeves down over my hands. "She's been in the house since we moved here. I'm sure of it. She even said as much last night." Annie and Tamela echo my shiver with their own.

Lucy inches up to the edge of her seat. "I've talked to everyone associated with any possible sale of the marina, and it was never a go. Of course, I wonder how many would have said that last week." She widens her eyes and crosses her legs, straightening her tennis skirt as she continues. "Pierson was making all kinds of side deals using the York name, but mostly he was trying to get his mother off his back by getting her the house. I guess he'd finally had enough that day on the boat and told her Saundra had found out and it was all off. At that point he was just trying to save his own scalp, but she hit him with the pitcher and walked away."

Greyson says, "It's still to be determined if she knew he fell over at the time. We didn't know she was even in town. I suppose her using your house and property let her come and go without people noticing." He shrugs and looks at me. "She does say she's been in the house since you've owned it, but who knows. She's saying a lot that doesn't make sense. But I guess with that window being so accessible, she could've."

Several arched eyebrows fly in Craig's direction. He swallows and gives me a look of apology, then says, "I thought of this last night. Ray

Barnette told me not to worry about who was in my office, that they didn't mean anything. So, did he know it was Leigh Anne Mantelle?"

Aiden drops his head and stares at his feet for a second. Then he peeks up at his mother and says, "Yeah, that's about it. Guess they go way back."

Annie huffs and settles herself with her mouth tight in a straight line.

Aiden looks at Craig. "He feels real bad about it. He just didn't see her as a threat to anyone. He actually thought the murderer was Sheryl-Lee. He said he followed you, Mr. Mantelle, and uh," he pauses and looks at me, "uh, Miss King the other night but nothing happened."

I smile at him. "No worries, Officer Bryant. I was following all of them that night!" That gets a laugh for a moment, but it fades out quickly.

Craig straightens up and speaks to Officer Greyson. "This does mean I'm free to leave town, correct?" At the officer's nod, Craig relaxes. "Good. Our permits all came through, and it's going to be a busy week at work." He takes a sip of coffee and adds nonchalantly, "Might need to go on down there later today to catch up."

Annie lays her hand on my thigh and squeezes it, but no one says anything for a few moments.

I lean to the side and pluck a small piece of the plant growing all along the railing. "So this is what jasmine smells like?" I take a deep breath. "I can see what all the fuss is about. It's delightful."

Tamela shudders, then stands quickly and begins to collect the trash. "I just don't know what this world is coming to. Sure, it's a nice house, but to kill for it?" With her hands full, she stops and looks around at the early morning light coming across the yard. "I'm glad y'all moved this furniture out here for this morning. It's a true spring day."

Lucy agrees. "What we call chamber of commerce weather. Can't wait to get on the tennis court before the spring weather is gone!"

"Spring gone?" I sputter. "But spring is officially still a week away."

Cherry laughs as she stands and stretches. "You'll get used to it eventually. Spring here usually starts somewhere in February and ends too soon. Now, I've got to go home and get in bed." She leans down to hug me. "I'm glad you're okay, but you take care of yourself. You're probably going to need to talk to a counselor later. You really had a traumatic experience."

Annie pats my knee. "I think she's right. That was pretty scary. Not exactly the cleanest solving of a case, but we did wrap it up pretty neatly." She swings around to look at both officers, whose eyes have popped open in alarm. "Don't you think so?"

Officer Greyson shakes his head. "No, I don't. It was a very dangerous situation you two were in." He turns his back on a frowning Annie and speaks to Craig. "Detective Johnson will still want to talk to you, I'm sure, so check with him before you leave town." He unfolds and comes to his feet. "I also need to go. I'm reporting in a bit later this morning due to last night. Thanks for the coffee and the baked goods. Officer Bryant, I'll see you at the station."

The officers take their leave as Craig carries a tray of dirty cups inside. Annie calls Cherry's name before she can head out.

"Wait a minute." Annie looks around the circle of us, a group of five unassuming, middle-aged (and more) ladies, her eyes wide and as sparkling as her silver curls in the morning sun. "I don't care what they say, girls. We solved this mystery. Sophia Island is lucky to have us, so keep your eyes open! You never know what you might see!"

CPSIA information can be obtained
at www.ICGtesting.com
Printed in the USA
BVHW080731070622
639019BV00001B/2